NICHOLAS GOADE, DETECTIVE

THE WORKS OF

E. PHILLIPS OPPENHEIM

NICHOLAS GOADE, DETECTIVE

WILDSIDE PRESS

CONTENTS

INTRODUCTION

Meet E. Phillips Oppenheim

Edward Phillips Oppenheim (1866-1946) was an Englishman, born in London, the son of a leather merchant. For twenty years he worked in his father's business, while beginning to publish novels. His first, subsidized by his father, barely broke even, but before long he was successful, enough so that a rich admirer, also in the leather business, bought out the firm and put Oppenheim on salary to support his writing career. Oppenheim soon hit his stride and became a bestseller, one of the most popular writers of his generation. He produced one hundred and sixteen novels and thirty-nine collections of short stories. At least twenty-one films were produced from his work, mostly in the silent era, including three versions of his most popular work, *The Great Impersonation.*

Oppenheim's specialty was the fast-moving, glamorous suspense thriller, written in a breezy, easy-to-read style. He was the epitome of the "entertainment" writer of his day, without any pretensions of literature. His stories are filled with high society people, spies, diplomats, and political intrigue, without much actual detection, so, it has been remarked, his relationship to the formal mystery story is slight. One difference between Oppenheim and many other writers who described glamorous high society was that he had actually been there. Once he was successful, he had a yacht and a villa on the French Riviera, where he spent his winters and moved in elite circles.

In his most famous work, *The Great Impersonation,* a German and an Englishman, who could be identical twins, meet together in Africa and note their uncanny resemblance. Then the German plots to make the Englishman disappear and steal his identity in order to carry on an espionage mission. The trick of the book is that the reader follows the man's return to England without ever knowing *which* man has returned. Is it the Englishman or the German impostor? Even those closest to him don't know.

Oppenheim was widely admired in his day. John Buchan, the author of *The Thirty-Nine Steps* called him "My master in fiction."

—Darrell Schweitzer
Philadelphia, Pennsylvania

NICHOLAS GOADE, DETECTIVE

I

THE CORONER'S DILEMMA

By the side of one of those winding byways which connect a few scattered hamlets upon the lower fringe of Exmoor with the important town of Market Bridgeford, a man stood painting an execrable water colour. A few yards away, drawn up in the shade of the high hedge, was an ancient Ford car; seated by the side of the man, and obviously bored with the whole proceeding, was a small, fat, white dog of the Sealyham type. The man had not the appearance of an artist, as indeed he was not. He was powerfully built, somewhat ruddy of complexion, with shrewd, blue eyes and an indomitable jaw. A physiognomy which might have been on the heavy side was redeemed by a humorous mouth. He had masses of dark brown hair — rather too much of it for careful arrangement — and the fingers which gripped his brush were the fingers of a sculptor rather than of a painter. His name was Nicholas Goade. He was thirty-eight years old, and he was enjoying his first long holiday — earned in somewhat singular fashion — since he joined the force. A month earlier he had arrested single-handed a criminal who for five years had de-

fied the police of New York and London, and had
simultaneously been handed a cheque for twenty-
five thousand dollars from the former and six
months' leave of absence from English headquar-
ters. Hence this long-planned vacation.

Suddenly the peace of the early summer afternoon was curiously disturbed. Flip, the first to
realise the approach of the unusual, sat up with a
short, warning bark. Goade turned his head, and,
with his hand shading his eyes, gazed down the
road. A riderless horse was galloping towards
them, the thunder of its hoofs becoming each second
more distinct. In the far distance, where the road
wound its way in to the hills again after a short dis-
appearance in the valley, was a little cloud of dust.
There was no other sign of life or movement in this
dreaming landscape.

Nicholas Goade thrust his precious canvas into
the car and stood for a moment in the middle of the
road without any very clear idea as to his course of
action. He was a humane man, but he was also a
man of common sense, and he had no intention of
risking his life or even a serious injury for the sake
of a runaway horse who would probably come to a
standstill of its own accord as soon as its energies
were spent. As a matter of fact, action on his part
became unnecessary. The horse, as soon as it
caught sight of him, slackened speed, looked
around for a moment nervously, and then came on

at a walk. It was still terrified, its ears laid back, its coat bathed in sweat, the stirrups jangling against its heaving sides; but it seemed to recognise in the man who confronted it a soothing influence. Goade patted its streaming neck, examined the great weal down its flank, led it on to the turf by the side of the road, and then, climbing into his car, drove in the direction from which the runaway had come.

About half a mile back, on the edge of the common which skirted the road, he came to the spot from which the animal had apparently started. The figure of a man in ordinary riding clothes was lying stretched upon the turf, face downwards and motionless. Goade bent over him, and, accustomed though he was to terrible sights, he felt a little surge of horror at the nature of the injuries to the man's head and neck. He returned to the car, fetched his rug, and, after another glance at the prostrate figure, covered it over. Then, with the instinct which belonged to his profession, he looked around for signs of some struggle between the man and the horse. He was puzzled to find none. The turf was nowhere cut up and, soft and yielding though it was, bore only the imprints of the lightest of hoof marks. The scene of the tragedy was a little inlet of turf, surrounded by gorse bushes — an inlet on to which the horse had presumably turned from the road for some reason. About

twenty yards away was a small shed — apparently
a shepherd's shelter.   There was no human being
in sight, nor sign of any vehicle.   Goade bent once
more over the man's body and felt it with a prac-
tised hand.   It was still warm.   Death could only
have taken place a few minutes before.   He turned
round at the sound of horse's hoofs, slow now and
faltering.   The animal had followed him up the
hill, and, after standing for a moment shivering on
the edge of the road, advanced slowly, whinnied,
and thrust its head down as though it recognised
its prostrate master.   Goade examined once more
the weal on its side, patted its neck gently, and
climbed on to a small hillock.   The little cloud of
dust on the ribbon of road skirting the hillside had
vanished.   There was no sign anywhere of pedes-
trian or vehicle.   After a few moment's reflection,
he slipped off his shoes, led the horse quietly to the
other side of the road, and commenced a closer ex-
amination of the little semicircle of turf upon which
the accident seemed to have happened.   In a
quarter of an hour's time he stood upright again
and looked around.   There was still no sign anywhere of the assistance which was necessary before
he could move the dead man.   He put on his shoes
and made his way along the narrow path towards
the shed.

Soon after the little cloud of dust upon the hillside had vanished, George Unwin turned in at the drive of his pleasantly situated, small country home, brought his car to a standstill at the front door, and rang the outside bell which would summon the chauffeur from the garage. He paused for a moment, drawing off his gloves and looking around him as though enjoying the prospect — a pleasant one enough: a vision of a trimly kept lawn with a paddock behind, a profusion of flowers, everywhere signs of well-being and comfort. Humming lightly to himself, he felt one of the back tyres and gave instructions concerning it to the chauffeur, who came hurrying up from the garage. Afterwards he nodded pleasantly to the parlourmaid who had opened the door in response to his ring, laid his hat and gloves upon the hall table, and, still humming under his breath, strolled with his habitual air of dignified composure into the room which was given over to him as a study. There was nothing in his manner to denote that within the last quarter of an hour he had committed a brutal murder.

"Is your mistress in, Rose?" he enquired.

"The mistress is resting, sir," the maid replied. "She ordered the little car for this afternoon, but changed her mind. She was complaining of a headache after lunch."

Her master nodded.

"I think I'll have a whisky and soda," he decided. "Bring me the things and I'll help myself."

The maid hastened to obey, and George Unwin mixed himself a drink with steady fingers. Nevertheless, as soon as the girl had departed, he doubled the quantity of whisky and drank half the contents of the tumbler at a gulp. Afterwards he stood and looked at himself carefully in the mirror. There were no signs of any disturbance either in his face, his attire, or the prim arrangement of his collar and tie. He was dressed — as became a respectable solicitor with a large practice — neatly and with a certain decorum which might be taken as a tribute to his profession. His tie was arranged almost as a stock, his collar, spotlessly white, a trifle higher than was altogether customary for country wear. His clothes were of dark serge, quietly fashioned and well fitting. He continued to examine himself with the utmost care. His black hair was unruffled, his eyes perhaps a little brighter than usual, and there was even a faint tinge of colour in his ordinarily pallid cheeks. Satisfied with his scrutiny, he approached a bookshelf, and, withdrawing a volume entitled "Practical Criminology" from a selected series dealing with the same subject, seated himself in an easy-chair and buried himself in its contents. He knew the exact chapter of which he was in search, and turned to it eagerly — a chapter containing the confessions of a criminal who had planned a murder for three months, planned and thought out every detail with scientific accuracy, but through some strange chain of circumstances had left one single clue. He devoured the few pages, then, half closing the book, with his finger in the place, gave himself up to thought. Was there anything that he had done or left undone? One by one he went over the events of the afternoon. He had left his office in the neighbouring market town earlier than usual, it was true, but during the summer months this was by no means an unusual occurrence. No one had seen him turn off the main road which would have been the quickest route to his abode, nor had he encountered a single soul along that stretch of lonely byway where, somewhere or other, he knew that he would meet the man whom he sought. They had come together just as he had planned and desired, within a few yards of the shed. He went over in memory the brief words which had passed between them, then the sudden throwing away of the hypocrisy of years, the lurid outburst when once he was sure of his man, the restrained passion of months, blazing in a torrent of words, nerving his arm to that unforgettable deed. It had been almost easier than he had expected. Even a strong man, half stunned, is not so very difficult to kill. George Unwin sat in his chair and gloated. The silent hatred of those miserable months, so well concealed, had spent itself in those wild moments. He became more and more exultant. He told himself that he had made no mistake, that he was safe, and that that silent, gnawing agony at which no one had guessed, which had made his life a hell, had gone. It was early days yet for the new horror to be born.

There was the sound of light footsteps in the hall, and his fingers stiffened upon the volume which he was holding. He threw it down upon the table just as the door opened and his wife entered. He half rose to his feet as he greeted her. His manners were always precise.

"You're home early, George," she remarked.

He nodded.

"There was very little doing at the office. I hope Rose is going to give us tea in the garden."

"Of course she can."

He watched her covertly as she stood with her finger upon the bell. She was a woman of negative complexion, with a graceful figure, lips unusually scarlet, and eyes of elusive colour. She had the air of being a foreigner, although, as a matter of fact, she had been born and lived most of her life in the neighbouring village. As he watched her he remembered some of the legends of the Spaniards who had made a settlement in the vicinity hundreds of years ago. Without a doubt there was foreign blood in her — perhaps in him too.

He felt very unEnglish this afternoon. He felt very unlike George Unwin, Esquire, of Unwin, Brooks & Calvert, solicitors, Clerk to the County Council, Under Sheriff of the County, the holder of many other public offices. That legend of foreign blood was probably true, or George Unwin, so much respected as the embodiment of legal distinction and upright living, would never have felt the fierce joy he was feeling at that moment.

"I thought perhaps that I should find you motoring," he remarked.

"I don't go out every afternoon," she answered carelessly.

A lie, he told himself. He knew — for days he had known — all about those picnic luncheons, little excursions to the wood, the telephone first to his office to be sure of his movements. He knew very well why he had found her at home that afternoon. From the extension to his office he had listened to her casual enquiry outside to the clerks, heard the reply given according to his instructions — "Mr. Unwin will be coming home early." It had been necessary to keep her out of the way that afternoon. Would she ever guess? he wondered.

She gave him tea in the shade of the cedar tree, and they spoke of indifferent things — their neighbours, a coming tennis tournament. Then, without a tremor in his voice, he introduced the name of the man who was lying dead by the roadside.

"Seen anything of Sir Michael the last few days?"

She shook her head.

"How should I?" she asked. "He very seldom calls unless you are here."

"Liar!" he thought to himself. He studied her with a new and strange interest. Such perfect deceit was in itself an attribute of the science which for years had been his hobby. What a criminal she herself would have made. Perhaps if he had not discovered her secret by the merest chance, he might himself have been her victim. A woman who could deceive like that could also kill.

"Shall we walk down to the hayfield?" she suggested. "Crask says that we shall have quite a crop."

He strolled along by her side, smoking the cigarette which he usually lit after tea — the one cigarette which was to last him until dinner time. Again they spoke of indifferent matters, pleasantly and with no apparent lack of interest. No one could have guessed at the wall between them, the wall which he had seen growing day by day in ever-deepening despair. Now and then, as they paraded their little domain — the domain, he reflected, where they were to spend the rest of their lives together — he looked down the drive and along the road. The postman came and went without news, a baker delivered bread, a motor-

cyclist friend waved a casual greeting.   After all,
it was a lonely spot where the man lay dead!

He dressed for dinner with slow deliberation,
studying himself the while in the mirror.   He had
a long, lean face, not unpleasing, although his
cheeks were a little sunken — not the face of a
murderer, he thought, as he arranged his tie.
That was a thing no one would ever believe of him.
Well, no one would ever know it.   He smiled
grimly to himself as he thought of the future —
thought of himself fulfilling with dignity all the
various offices of the law, a well-respected man in
his world, a trifle austere and parchmentlike perhaps, in his dealing with human beings; certainly
not a person to be suspected of temper, of passion,
of the courage which arms a man's will to kill.
There was scarcely a soul in the county who would
not have laughed at the idea of numbering him
amongst that ghostly little company who had qual-
ified for the scaffold — some of whom had walked
those few fatal steps, and some who had escaped.
He belonged there, all right, but nobody would ever
know.

At dinner time and afterwards the devil entered
into George Unwin.   He ordered champagne, and
he talked to his wife as he had not talked for months
past, not since he had guessed, not since he had
known.   He watched her growing uneasiness —
realised, too, that it made her more beautiful.

Afterwards they walked in the garden together. His arm went around her waist. He took her hand in his, and, notwithstanding the warmth of the June evening, her fingers seemed icy cold. A nightingale sang, and they paused to listen. He could feel her trembling in his grasp. A torturer's sense seemed born in him in those few moments. He found no pleasure in holding her to him, in the kiss he forced from her shrinking lips, yet he played the expectant lover and felt a horrible joy in her sufferings. In the house she escaped, but he followed her to her little drawing-room. Her respite came by terrible means. He knew what it meant, the ringing of the bell at that unexpected hour. Did she guess, he wondered, that something might have happened, for her eyes shone strangely as she listened to the heavy footsteps in the hall? Rose bustled in with an air of importance.

"The police sergeant would like to speak to you, sir," she announced.

Even then he would not spare her. Malice was ablaze in him that night.

"Ask the sergeant to step in," he directed carelessly.

The sergeant presented himself — a large man, excited and perspiring. He saluted Unwin with the deep respect due to the arch-representative of the law. He looked towards Mrs. Unwin and made mysterious signs.

"What is it, Sergeant?" Unwin asked.   "Speak up."

"It's a fair nasty business," the man answered, turning his cap over.   "I was thinking maybe the lady mightn't like to hear."

She leaned forward in her chair.

"Go on, Sergeant," she insisted.

"There's been a bad accident — a real bad 'un."

"Any one hurt?" Unwin asked.

"Who is it?" his wife demanded, in a whisper which seemed to crackle through the twilight of the room.

"It's Sir Michael, sir and lady," the man confided ponderously.   "Met with an accident while he was out riding, seemingly."

"Seriously hurt?" Unwin enquired.

The sergeant shook his head.

"He were stone dead when they found him, sir. A tourist gentleman from London had been sitting by the body for an hour and more, waiting for some-one to pass.   It were down on the Cudfield Lane, where not many do find their way."

George Unwin held a glass of water to his wife's lips, but she waved it away.   She was deathly pale, but she showed no signs of fainting.

"You mean that he is dead, Sergeant?"

"That sure-ly is so," the man admitted reluctantly.   "And a terrible thing for all of us, for a better man or landlord never was.   He must have fell on his head, they reckon, and that bay mare of his got obstreperous and kicked him as he lay."

"This is terrible news," George Unwin said, wondering at the solemnity of his own tone. "Where have they taken the body, Sergeant?"

"That's just what I'm here for to know your wishes, Mr. Unwin. A farm wagon was all that come along, and they moved 'un to the Red Cow at Cudfield, and laid 'un in the parlour there. The inspector, he sent me up right away to know if you'd any special wish about the inquest, or if it could be held there."

For a single moment Unwin almost lost control of himself. Strange, with his perfect memory, his grasp of detail, his careful consideration of all that had happened, of all that might happen, he had forgotten one thing — he was the coroner, and it was his office to send this man to his grave! . . . When he spoke, however, it was after not undue hesitation, though he scarcely recognised his own voice. It seemed to come to him from a long way off.

"The body had better remain where it is," he directed. "The inquest can be held in the market room at the inn."

The sergeant took his leave and departed under the escort of the parlourmaid for entertainment in the kitchen. George Unwin and his wife were left alone in the room. It seemed to have grown darker during the last few minutes.   Unwin bent over the lamp.   He was stopped by his wife's staccato cry.

"Don't do that, George. I can't bear it. Listen! Turn towards me.   I want to see your face."

He turned around without hesitation, even with deliberation.   Their eyes met: hers afire with passionate, hysterical questioning, his face a mask.

"You knew?" she faltered.

"Be reasonable," he answered.   "How was it possible?   Besides, why should I have kept it from you all this time?"

She said nothing more.   Presently she looked away from him.   She seemed to be gazing through the walls, and there was a horror in her face which awed him in spite of himself.   He moved uncomfortably about.

"You take this hardly, Julia," he said.   "He was an old friend and neighbour, of course, but, after all, we saw very little of him."

She made no reply.   There was something about her dumbness which for the first time brought a tremor of icy fear into his heart.

George Unwin had never more perfectly embodied the dignity and sufficiency of the law than at the inquest over which, in due course, he presided.   It was he himself who, in the little room where the remains of the dead man had been placed, drew the sheet from his face, and, with the doctor by his side, explained the injuries. In his seat at the head of the long table in the market room afterwards, his grave, sympathetic voice seemed almost to have attained a new note of humanity.

"This is a case, gentlemen," he said, glancing down at the little company — five farmers, one gamekeeper, a retired school-master, a labourer, and village tradespeople — "which will, I think, present no difficulties to you. The doctor will tell you that the injuries from which our dearly loved and respected neighbour died were undoubtedly caused by the iron shoe of a horse. How Sir Michael came to be thrown, we shall unfortunately never know, but it seems to me most probable that his horse stumbled, that they both fell, and that the kicking took place without any viciousness on the part of the animal whilst it was struggling to regain its feet. That, however, must remain a matter of speculation. It is just one of those terrible accidents which happen sometimes and for which we cannot altogether account. We were to have had here as a witness the gentlemen who discovered the body, but I imagine that he will have little further light to throw upon what has happened. Your verdict will naturally be one of 'Accidental Death', and I trust that you will add to it the customary expression of condolence with the relatives of the deceased."

There was a subdued murmur of acquiescence.

" 'Accidental Death' it be, sure enough," one of the farmers observed, "and a cruel, unlucky thing. It do seem a queer business to me, though, that Sir Michael should have been thrown.   He were a rare 'un on a horse."

"What probably happened," Unwin pointed out, "was that the animal, startled by something in the lane, shied sideways on to the little piece of turf where the body was found.   He probably stumbled in mounting from the lane — there is a slight incline — and then fell.   The finest horseman in the world can do nothing with a stumbling horse."

"That be true, sir," one of the farmers agreed.

"What about the gentleman as found the body? Us'd like to have seen him," someone else interposed.

"He was summoned to the inquest," Unwin explained, "and, as you know, we waited ten minutes for him.   It seemed scarcely worth while, in view of the fact that he can have nothing fresh to tell us, to adjourn, but, if you gentlemen wish it, we can easily do so.   I am only anxious not to take up another afternoon just about harvest time."

There was the sound of a motor horn outside. George Unwin looked up quickly.   To him there was a note of something sinister in its shrill hooting. His composure, however, never wavered.

"Perhaps this is our missing witness," he said, leaning back in his chair.

There was a moment's silence, and then a knock at the door, which was opened by the police sergeant. Nicholas Goade entered, followed by a tall, slight man of military appearance.

"Here be Chief Constable," one of the farmers whispered, nudging his neighbour. "What be he wanting, I wonder?"

The coroner greeted the newcomers with dignity, and chairs were provided for them.

"We have been hoping for your evidence, sir," he remarked, addressing Nicholas Goade. "You were summoned for two-thirty."

"I must offer my apologies," was the quiet reply. "I was told three-thirty. In any case ——"

He broke off and turned towards his companion. The Chief Constable whispered in Unwin's ear, and there was silence for several moments in the room. Unwin inclined his head once or twice as though in sympathy with the words to which he was listening. Once he half-started and glanced towards Goade. At no other time did his face betray the slightest emotion. Finally he turned to the jury.

"Gentlemen," he said, "Captain Faulkener here has laid before me certain facts which I think should be investigated. He points out that you have not had an opportunity of visiting the scene of this terrible accident. Personally I admit that I scarcely thought it necessary, but, as Captain Faulkener thinks otherwise, I am afraid I must trouble you to make the journey. Would to-morrow afternoon be suitable?"

There was a murmur of assent.

"Then let it be to-morrow," Unwin decided. "Conveyances shall be here at the inn at two o'clock. That is agreeable to you also, Captain Faulkener?"

"Perfectly," the Chief Constable replied. "I am sorry to have to interfere in the matter at all, Unwin. It certainly seems a clear enough case, but there are one or two minor points which I think had better be cleared up. Our friend Mr. Goade here must be considered."

"It is my wish," George Unwin concluded, with a dignified little bow, "to conduct these proceedings strictly according to the law and with due consideration to any theories which you gentlemen may have to advance. Gentlemen of the Jury, I need not detain you longer. The inquest is adjourned until two o'clock to-morrow afternoon."

There was nothing to call George Unwin to his office in Market Bridgeford that afternoon, but on leaving the inquest he deliberately made his way there instead of homeward. He sat in his private room, transacting insignificant business until the last of his clerks, with an apologetic cough, ventured to suggest that the hour for closing had arrived. At the Crown Hotel, where his car stood in the yard, he entered the bar parlour amidst many respectful salutations, and drank a glass of old sherry.   He was a person of consequence in the little company, and was treated as such.   The general topic of interest naturally enough was the adjourned inquest.   He waved the subject away with a gesture of depreciation when it was mooted.

"After to-morrow," he told them, "we can discuss the matter.   Until then '*sub judice*.'   You understand?"

No one understood, but they shook their heads solemnly.   Presently he lit a cigarette, and departed amidst a chorus of friendly farewells — a man highly thought of amongst them all, a man who upheld the dignity of the law, taking his place with the Bank, the Church, and the Squire amidst the Forces of the County. . . .   He reached home only a short time before dinner.   Again he scrutinised his face as he leaned towards the mirror to straighten his tie.   Was it his fancy, he wondered, or were there really shadows under his eyes?   The heat, he told himself.   It had been a trying day, and that sudden break in the middle of the inquest was, to say the least of it, disturbing.   He would have liked that verdict of "Accidental Death" safely recorded.

Julia was late for dinner — wandering in the garden, it seemed — he wondered whether with the object of avoiding him?   During the service of the meal they spoke only of the heat, the crop of hay, the roses.   Afterwards he felt suddenly weary.

He had no longer the enterprise for wandering through the gardens, or the devilment for playing the torturer. He sat on a seat under the cedar tree and sipped his coffee. His wife, after a few minutes' hesitation, seated herself by his side. It was not, however, until the twilight deepened that she spoke.

"Is it all over?" she asked.

"No," he answered. "The inquest is adjourned."

He heard the quick intake of her breath — a little stabbing sound through the silence.

"Adjourned? Why?"

He knocked the ash from his cigarette.

"Faulkener, the Chief Constable, arrived with the man who found the body just as the jury were giving their verdict. Faulkener thought it better that the jury should visit the spot. They are going there to-morrow afternoon."

"Who was this man who found him?" she enquired.

"His name, if I remember rightly, was Nicholas Goade. He called himself an artist."

A flash of summer lightning opened the sky. She gave a little moan.

"I think that there is a storm coming," she murmured.

"I too," he acquiesced. "Shall we move indoors?"

She shook her head.

"Tell me," she whispered, "what does this adjourned inquest really mean?"

Their eyes met. It seemed to him in that awful moment that each knew the other's secret.

"Simply a waste of time," he assured her briefly. "Nothing more will ever be known of the manner of Sir Michael's death than is known at this moment."

For a long time she sat in silence. A jagged tongue of black cloud crept across the sky. Once more the heavens opened, and this time the thunder followed. Large drops of rain fell upon them. He rose to his feet and held out his hand.

"Come along!" he insisted. "Quickly! You know that you are frightened of lightning. Come!"

She shrank still farther back in her chair, and he knew that it was no longer the lightning which she feared. He turned and left her. The rain, beating through her thin garments, wetted her to the skin. As soon as he had disappeared, she rose and made her way into the house by the back entrance.

There was a remarkable metamorphosis in the lonely Devonshire lane when, on the following afternoon, the four motor cars came sobbing up the hill and stopped opposite that semicircular piece of turf. A dozen policemen were there, holding a cord which enclosed seventy or eighty yards of common and included the shed. The members of the jury stood aimlessly about, looking down at the turf, still uncertain as to why they had been brought there. Captain Faulkener passed his arm through George Unwin's and drew him a little on one side.

"Before we go any further, Unwin," he said, "I think you'd better get a grip of this business. Our friend Goade here, who happened in upon this affair, is quite a famous detective from Scotland Yard — the man, by the by, who got the twenty-five thousand dollars' reward for arresting Ned Bullivant. He came over to see me yesterday morning and drew my attention to certain facts. I must confess that at first I was inclined to consider his theory ridiculous. In the end, however, he converted me."

"And what might be his theory?" George Unwin enquired, a little formally.

"In the first place," the other continued, "the wounds upon Sir Michael's head are of a somewhat curious shape. As Mr. Goade has pointed out, they appear to have been made by a horseshoe, but scarcely by the rear portion of it. He has instituted a thorough search amongst the gorse bushes around, and about twenty yards away one of the men whom I have detailed over here discovered a

loose horseshoe, upon which were marks of blood
at a spot exactly coinciding with the worst of the
wounds.   They found the horseshoe, as I told you,
about twenty yards away — just about the distance, you see, that a man might throw it from the
scene of the accident."

"You have the horseshoe?"

"Naturally.   It is there for production before
the jury.   Further, as Goade has also pointed out,
there is no sign whatever of the turf being cut up
by the struggling of a fallen horse.   On the other
hand, there are marks of two distinct sets of foot-
prints.   Sir Michael, too, notoriously never used
his whip, yet on the side of his mare there is to-day
— I have seen her in the stables — a tremendous
weal."

"Anything else?"

The Chief Constable nodded gravely.

"Goade made a thorough search of the place
whilst he was waiting.   You see that little shed?"

Unwin glanced at it and away again almost immediately.

"Well?"

"Underneath a stone there," the Chief Constable
confided, "I found this."

Unwin took the scrap of paper into his hand.
The words suddenly danced before his eyes.   The
sweat from his fingers smudged the ink.   He stared
at the four words scrawled on a half sheet of his

own notepaper, battling all the time with a sickly horror. His death warrant written in the frail caligraphy he knew so well!

"Be careful.   George suspects."

"From all this, as you may imagine," Captain Faulkener continued, glancing over his shoulder at the little group of men standing about in the sunlight, "Goade has elaborated a perfectly reasonable and, to my mind, convincing theory.   He found distinct traces of a car in the road which came just as far as here and no farther.   His theory is that Sir Michael — poor old Michael; we all know that his reputation was none of the best — has been making assignations here with some young woman of the neighbourhood.   Her husband or lover got jealous.   She took alarm and left this note for him in the shed, which was without a doubt their meeting place.   He came up as usual and found the husband or lover lying in wait.   The murderer, whoever he may be, attacked Sir Michael with this horseshoe, stunned him with it unexpectedly, deliberately killed him, struck his horse that terrible blow so that it should gallop off, and left him lying here, apparently the victim of an accident.   What do you think of that, Unwin?"

"Amazing!" was the toneless reply.   "Really, I must express my congratulations to Mr. Goade."

"Don't hurry for a moment," the Chief Constable begged. "He is showing the jury the shed. Here they come."

"They have seen now everything that is necessary," Unwin declared. "We will go back to the village and reopen the inquest. I must confess that in the light of all this my instructions to the jury were ill-founded. 'Wilful Murder against some Person or Persons Unknown' it will have to be this time, I'm afraid."

Captain Faulkener shook his head gravely. Glancing around, Unwin was suddenly aware that two of the attendant policemen had drawn a little closer to him. His hand disappeared for a moment into his waistcoat pocket, and afterwards his fingers rested upon his lips.

"Not necessarily unknown, I am afraid, Unwin," his companion said solemnly. "The writing on that slip of paper — your stationery, by the by — has already been identified as the writing of your wife. The marks of the car which drew up here have been traced to your drive. The blood-stained horseshoe throw into the gorse bushes was one you stopped to pick up just outside Cudfield village. This is a very painful duty for me, Unwin, but I am afraid I must ask you to consider yourself under arrest."

The handcuffs were on his wrists before he could move. He followed with his eyes the winding road through the valley and around the hills to where

he could catch a distant glimpse of his own house.
The road seemed suddenly to stagger before his
eyes. Two larks were singing directly above his
head. A puff of hay-scented breeze was wafted
across the road to mingle with the perfume of the
sun-warmed gorse and wild thyme. The skies began to dance. Inside he felt the breaking of the
waves. They were looking at him curiously now,
crowding up towards him — his jury! He summoned all his strength.

"Gentlemen of the Jury," he faltered, "your
verdict must be 'Wilful Murder against George
Unwin.' I killed him. Thank God I killed him!"

"A strange fellow," they decided at the Farmers'
Dinner on the following Saturday. "For five-and-
twenty years a stern, law-abiding, conscientious
official of the law, and then — a murderer!"

"Criminologically an amazingly interesting
study," his successor, the deputy coroner, declared.

"A drop of foreign blood somewhere," one of the
twelve jurymen insisted.

II

NICHOLAS GOADE was without doubt a very first-
class detective, but as a wayfarer across Devonshire byroads, with only a map and a compass to
help him, he was simply a "washout." Even his
fat little white dog, Flip, sheltered under a couple
of rugs, after two hours of cold, wet, and purpose-
less journeying, looked at him reproachfully.
With an exclamation of something like despair,
Goade brought his sobbing automobile to a standstill at the top of one of the wickedest hills a Ford
had ever been asked to face, even on first speed, and
sat looking around him. In every direction the
outlook was the same. There were rolling stretches
of common, divided by wooded valleys of incredible
depth. There was no sign of agricultural land, no
sign of the working of any human being upon the
endless acres, and not a single vehicle had he passed
upon the way. There were no signposts, no vil-
lages, no shelter of any sort. The one thing that
abounded was rain — rain and mist. Grey
wreaths of it hung over the commons, making them
seem like falling fragments of cloud, blotting out
the horizon; hung over every hopeful break in the

distance — an encircling, enveloping obscurity.
Then, vying with the mists in wetness, came the
level rain — rain which had seemed beautiful early
in the afternoon, slanting from the heavens on to
the mountainside, but rain which had long ago lost
all pretence to being anything but damnably offensive, chilling, miserably wet. Flip, whose nose
only now appeared uncovered, sniffed disgustedly,
and Goade, as he lit a pipe, cursed slowly but flu-
ently under his breath. What a country! Miles
of byways without a single signpost, endless
stretches without a glimpse of a farmhouse or village. And the map! Goade solemnly cursed the
man who had ordained it, the printer who had bound
it, and the shop where he had bought it. When
he had finished, Flip ventured upon a gentle bark
of approval.

"Somewhere or other," Goade muttered to himself, "should lie the village of Nidd. The last
signpost in this blasted region indicated six miles
to Nidd. Since then we have travelled at least
twelve, there has been no turning to the left or to
the right, and the village of Nidd is as though it
had never been."

His eyes pierced the gathering darkness ahead.
Through a slight uplifting in the clouds it seemed
to him that he could see for miles, and nowhere was
there any sign of village or of human habitation.
He thought of the road along which they had come,

and the idea of retracing it made him shiver. It
was at that moment, when bending forward to
watch the steam from his boiling radiator, that he
saw away on the left a feebly flickering light. Instantly he was out of the car. He scrambled on
to the stone wall and looked eagerly in the direction
from which he had seen it. There was, without
doubt, a light; around that light must be a house.
His eyes could even trace the rough track that led
to it. He climbed back to his place, thrust in his
clutch, drove for about forty yards, and then
paused at a gate. The track on the other side was
terrible, but then so was the road. He opened it
and drove through, bending over his task now with
every sense absorbed. Apparently traffic here, if
traffic existed at all, consisted only of an occasional
farm wagon of the kind he was beginning to know
all about — springless, with holes in the boarded
floor, and with great, slowly turning wheels.
Nevertheless, he made progress, skirted the edge of
a tremendous combe, passed, to his joy, a semi-
cultivated field, through another gate, up, it seemed
suddenly, into the clouds, and down a fantastic
corkscrew way until at last the light faced him
directly ahead. He passed a deserted garden,
pulled up before a broken-down iron gate, which
he had to descend and open, and which he punctili-
ously closed after him, traversed a few yards of
grass-grown, soggy avenue, and finally reached the

door of what might once have been a very tolerable farmhouse, but which appeared now, notwithstanding the flickering light burning upstairs, to be one of the most melancholy edifices the mind of man could conceive. With scant anticipations in the way of a welcome, but with immense relief at the thought of a roof, Goade descended and knocked upon the oak door. Inside he could hear almost at once the sound of a match being struck; the light of a candle shone through the blindless windows of a room on his left. There were footsteps in the hall, and the door was opened. Goade found himself confronted by a woman, who held the candle so high above her head that he was able to see little of her features. There was a certain stateliness, however, about her figure, which he realised even in those first few seconds.

"What do you want?" she asked.

Goade, as he removed his hat, fancied that the answer was sufficiently obvious. Rain streamed from every angle of his bemackintoshed body. His face was pinched with the cold.

"I am a traveller who has lost his way," he explained. "For hours I have been trying to find a village and inn. Yours is the first human habitation I have seen. Can you give me a night's shelter?"

"Is there any one with you?" the woman enquired.

"I am alone," he replied — "except for my little dog," he added, as he heard Flip's hopeful yap.

The woman considered.

"You had better drive your car into the shed on the left-hand side of the house," she said. "Afterwards you can come in. We will do what we can for you. It is not much."

"I am very grateful, madam," Goade declared in all sincerity.

He found the shed, which was occupied only by two farm carts in an incredible state of decay. Afterwards he released Flip and returned to the front door, which had been left open. Guided by the sound of crackling logs, he found his way into a huge stone kitchen. In a high-backed chair in front of the fire, seated with her hands upon her knees, but gazing eagerly towards the door as though watching for his coming, was another woman, also tall, a little past middle age perhaps, but still of striking presence and fine features. The woman who had admitted him was bending over the fire. He looked from one to the other in amazement. They were fearfully and wonderfully alike.

"It is very kind of you, ladies, to give us shelter," he began. "Flip! Behave yourself, Flip!"

A huge sheep dog had occupied the space in front of the fire. Flip without a moment's hesitation had run towards him, yapping fiercely. The dog, with an air of mild surprise, rose to his feet and looked enquiringly downwards. Flip insinuated herself into the vacant place, stretched herself out with an air of content, and closed her eyes.

"I must apologise for my little dog," Goade continued. "She is very cold."

The sheep dog retreated a few yards and sat on his haunches, considering the matter. Meanwhile the woman who had opened the door produced a cup and saucer from a cupboard, a loaf of bread, and a small side of bacon, from which she cut some slices.

"Draw your chair to the fire," she invited. "We have very little to offer you, but I will prepare something to eat."

"You are good Samaritans indeed," Goade declared fervently.

He seated himself opposite the woman who as yet had scarcely spoken or removed her eyes from his. The likeness between the two was an amazing thing, as was also their silence. They wore similar clothes — heavy, voluminous clothes they seemed to him — and each had a brooch at her bosom. Their hair, black and slightly besprinkled with grey, was arranged in precisely the same fashion. Their clothes belonged to another world, as did also their speech and manners, yet there was a curious distinction about them both.

"As a matter of curiosity," Goade asked, "how far am I from the village of Nidd?"

"Not far," the woman who was sitting motionless opposite to him answered. "To any one knowing the way, near enough. Strangers are foolish
to trust themselves to these roads. Many people
are lost who try."

"Yours is a lonely homestead," he ventured.

"We were born here," the woman answered.
"Neither my sister nor I have felt the desire for
travel."

The bacon began to sizzle. Flip opened one
eye, licked her mouth, and sat up. In a few minutes the meal was prepared. A high-backed, oak
chair was placed at the end of the table. There
was tea, a dish of bacon and eggs, a great loaf of
bread, and a small pot of butter. Goade took his
place.

"You have had your supper?" he asked.

"Long ago," the woman who had prepared his
meal replied. "Please to serve yourself."

She sank into the other oak chair exactly opposite her sister. Goade, with Flip by his side, commenced his meal. Neither had tasted food for
many hours, and for a time both were happily ob-
livious to anything save the immediate surroundings. Presently, however, as he poured out his
second cup of tea, Goade glanced towards his host-
esses. They had moved their chairs slightly away
from the fire and were both watching him — watching him without curiosity, yet with a certain puz-

zling intentness. It occurred to him then for the
first time that, although both had in turn addressed
him, neither had addressed the other.

"I can't tell you how good this tastes," Goade
said presently. "I am afraid I must seem awfully
greedy."

"You have been for some time without food, perhaps," one of them said.

"Since half-past twelve."

"Are you travelling for pleasure?"

"I thought so before to-day," he answered, with
a smile to which there was no response.

The woman who had admitted him moved her
chair an inch or two nearer to his. He noticed
with some curiosity that immediately she had done
so her sister did the same thing.

"What is your name?"

"Nicholas Goade," he replied. "May I know
whom I have to thank for this hospitality?"

"My name is Mathilda Craske," the first one
announced.

"And mine is Annabelle Craske," the other
echoed.

"You live here alone?" he ventured.

"We live here entirely alone," Mathilda acquiesced. "It is our pleasure."

Goade was more than ever puzzled. Their
speech was subject to the usual Devonshire intona-
tion and soft slurring of the vowels, but otherwise

it was almost curiously correct. The idea of their living alone in such a desolate part, however, seemed incredible.

"You farm here, perhaps?" he persisted. "You have labourers' cottages, or some one close at hand?"

Mathilda shook her head.

"The nearest hovel," she confided, "is three miles distant. We have ceased to occupy ourselves with the land. We have five cows — they give us no trouble — and some fowls."

"It is a lonely life," he murmured.

"We do not find it so," Annabelle said stiffly.

He turned his chair towards them. Flip, with a little gurgle of satisfaction, sprang on to his knees.

"Where do you do your marketing?" he asked.

"A carrier from Exford," Mathilda told him, "calls every Saturday. Our wants are simple."

The large room, singularly empty of furniture, as he noticed, looking round, was full of shadowy places, unillumined by the single oil lamp. The two women themselves were only dimly visible. Yet every now and then, in the flickering firelight, he caught a clearer glimpse of them. They appeared to him to be between forty and fifty years of age, so uncannily alike that they might well be twins. He found himself speculating as to their history. They must once have been very beautiful.

"I wonder whether it will be possible," he asked, after a somewhat prolonged pause, "to encroach further upon your hospitality and beg for a sofa or a bed for the night? Any place will do," he added hastily.

Mathilda rose at once to her feet. She took another candle from the mantelpiece and lit it.

"I will show you," she said, "where you may sleep."

For a moment Goade was startled. He had happened to glance towards Annabelle, and was amazed at a sudden curious expression — an expression almost of malice in her face. He stooped to bring her into the little halo of lamplight more completely and stared at her incredulously. The expression, if ever it had been there, had vanished. She was simply looking at him patiently, with something in her face which he failed utterly to understand.

"If you will follow me," Mathilda invited.

Goade rose to his feet. Flip turned round with a final challenging bark to the huge sheep dog, who had accepted a position remote from the fire, and, failing to elicit any satisfactory response, trotted after her master. They passed into a well-shaped but almost empty hall, up a broad flight of oak stairs, on to the first landing. Outside the room from which Goade had seen the candlelight she paused for a moment and listened.

"You have another guest?" he enquired.

"Annabelle has a guest," she replied.   "You are
mine.   Follow me, please."

She led the way to a bedchamber in which was a
huge four-poster and little else.   She set the candle
upon a table and turned down a sort of crazy quilt
which covered the bedclothes.   She felt the sheets
and nodded approvingly.   Goade found himself
unconsciously following her example.   To his surprise they were warm.   She pointed to a great
brass bed-warmer with a long handle at the farther
end of the room, from which a little smoke was still
curling upwards.

"You were expecting some one to-night?" he
asked curiously.

"We are always prepared," she answered.

She left the room, apparently forgetting to wish
him good night.   He called out pleasantly after
her, but she made no response.   He heard her level
footsteps as she descended the stairs.   Then again
there was silence — silence down below, silence in
the part of the house where he was.   Flip, who was
sniffing round the room, at times showed signs of
excitement, at times growled.   Goade, opening the
window, ventured upon a cigarette.

"Don't know that I blame you, old girl," he said.
"It's a queer place."

Outside there was nothing to be seen, and little
to be heard, save the roaring of a water torrent
close at hand and the patter of rain.   He suddenly

remembered his bag, and, leaving the door of his room open, descended the stairs. In the great stone kitchen the two women were seated exactly as they had been before his coming and during his meal. They both looked at him, but neither spoke.

"If you don't mind," he explained, "I want to fetch my bag from the car."

Mathilda, the woman who had admitted him, nodded acquiescence. He passed out into the darkness, stumbled his way to the shed, and un-strapped his bag. Just as he was turning away, he thrust his hand into the tool chest and drew out an electric torch, which he slipped into his pocket. When he reëntered the house, the two women were still seated in their chairs and still silent.

"A terrible night," he remarked. "I can't tell you how thankful I am to you for this shelter."

They both looked at him, but neither made any reply. This time, when he reached his room, he closed the door firmly, and noticed with a frown of disappointment that except for the latch there was no means of fastening it. Then he laughed to himself softly. He, the famous captor of Ned Bulli-vant, the victor in a score of scraps with desperate men, suddenly nervous in this lonely farmhouse in-habited by a couple of strange women.

"Time I took a holiday," he muttered to himself. "We don't understand nerves, do we, Flip?" he added, lifting the bedcover.

Flip opened one eye and growled. Goade was puzzled.

"Something about she doesn't like," he ruminated. "I wonder who's in the room with the lighted candles?"

He opened his own door once more softly and listened. The silence was almost unbroken. From downstairs in the great kitchen he could hear the ticking of a clock, and he could see the thin streak of yellow light underneath the door. He crossed the landing and listened for a moment outside the room with the candles. The silence within was absolute and complete — not even the sound of the ordinary breathing of a sleeping person. He retraced his steps, closed his own door, and began to undress. At the bottom of his bag was a small automatic. His fingers played with it for a moment. Then he threw it back. The electric torch, however, he placed by the side of his bed. Before he turned in, he leaned once more out of the window. The roar of the falling water seemed more insistent than ever. Otherwise there was no sound. The rain had ceased, but the sky was black and starless. With a little shiver, he turned away and climbed into bed.

He had no idea of the time, but the blackness outside was just as intense, when he was suddenly awakened by Flip's low growling. She had shaken herself free from the coverlet at the foot of the bed, and he could see her eyes, wicked little spots of light, gleaming through the darkness. He lay quite still for a moment, listening. From the first he knew that there was some one in the room. His own quick intuition had told him that, although he was still unable to detect a sound. Slowly his hand travelled out to the side of the bed. He took up the electric torch and turned it on. Then, with a little cry, he shrank back. Standing within a few feet of him was Mathilda, still fully dressed, and in her hand, stretched out towards him, was the cruellest-looking knife he had ever seen. He slipped out of bed, and, honestly and self-confessedly afraid, kept the light fixed upon her.

"What do you want?" he demanded, amazed at the unsteadiness of his own voice. "What the mischief are you doing with that knife?"

"I want you, William," she answered, a note of disappointment in her tone. "Why do you keep so far away?"

He lit the candle. The finger which, on the trigger of his automatic, had kept Bullivant with his hands up for a life-long two minutes, was trembling. With the light in the room now established, however, he felt more himself.

"Throw that knife on the bed," he ordered, "and tell me what you were going to do with it?"

She obeyed at once and leaned a little towards him.

"I was going to kill you, William," she confessed.

"And why?" he demanded.

She shook her head sorrowfully.

"Because it is the only way," she replied.

"My name isn't William, for one thing," he objected, "and what do you mean by saying it is the only way?"

She smiled, sadly and disbelievingly.

"You should not deny your name," she said. "You are William Foulsham. I knew you at once, though you had been away so long. When *he* came," she added, pointing towards the other room, "Annabelle believed that he was William. I let her keep him. I knew if I waited, you would come."

"Waiving the question of my identity," he struggled on, "why do you want to kill me? What do you mean by saying it is the only way?"

"It is the only way to keep men," she answered. "Annabelle and I found that out when William left us. We sat here and we waited for him to come back. We said nothing, but we both knew."

"You mean that you were going to kill me to keep me here?" he persisted.

She looked towards the knife lovingly.

"That isn't killing," she said. "Death wouldn't come till later on, and you could never go away. You would be there always."

He began to understand, and a horrible idea stole into his brain.

"What about the man she thought was William?" he asked.

"You shall see him if you like," she answered eagerly. "You shall see how peaceful and happy he is. Perhaps you will be sorry then that you woke up. Come with me."

He possessed himself of the knife and followed her out of the room and across the landing. Underneath the door he could see the little chink of light — the light which had been his beacon from the road. She opened the door softly and held the candle over her head. Stretched upon another huge four-poster bed was the figure of a man with a ragged, untidy beard. His face was as pale as the sheet, and Goade knew from the first glance that he was dead. By his side, seated stiffly in a high-backed chair, was Annabelle. She raised her finger and frowned as they entered. She looked across at Goade.

"Step quietly," she whispered. "William is asleep."

Just as the first gleam of dawn was forcing a finger of light through the sullen bank of clouds, a distraught and dishevelled-looking man, followed by a small, fat, white dog, stumbled into the village of Nidd, gasped with relief at the sight of the brass plate upon a door, and pulled the bell for all he was worth. Presently a window was opened and a man's shaggy head thrust out.

"Steady there!" he expostulated. "What's wrong?"

Goade looked up.

"I've spent a part of the night in a farmhouse a few miles from here," he explained. "There's a dead man there and two mad women, and my car's broken down."

"A dead man?" the doctor repeated.

"I've seen him. My car's broken down in the road, or I should have been here before."

"I'll be with you in five minutes," the doctor promised.

He was as good as his word. Presently they were seated in his car on their way back to the farm. He listened to Goade's story and nodded sympathetically.

"If the way I've been piecing it together turns out to be right," he remarked, "you've had a narrow escape."

It was light now and showed signs of clearing, and in a short time they drew up in front of the farmhouse. There was no answer to their knock. The doctor turned the handle of the door and opened it. They entered the kitchen. The fire was out, but, each in her high-backed chair, Mathilda and Annabelle were seated, facing each other, speechless, yet with wide-open eyes. They both turned their heads as the two men entered. Annabelle nodded slowly with satisfaction.

"It is the doctor," she said.   "Doctor, I am glad
that you have come.   You know, of course, that
William is back.   He came for me.   He is lying
upstairs, but I cannot wake him.   I sit with him
and I hold his hand and I speak to him, but he says
nothing.   He sleeps so soundly.   Will you wake
him for me, please.   I will show you where he lies."

She led the way from the room, and the doctor
followed her.   Mathilda listened to their footsteps.
Then she turned to Goade with that strange smile
once more upon her lips.

"Annabelle and I do not speak," she explained.
"We have not spoken for so many years that I forget how long it is.   I should like some one to tell
her, though, that the man who lies upstairs is not
William.   I should like some one to tell her that
you are William, and that you have come back for
me.   Sit down, William.   Presently, when the
doctor has gone, I will build the fire and make you
some tea."

Goade sat down, and again he felt his hands
trembling.   The woman looked at him kindly.

"You have been gone a long time," she continued.
"I should have known you anywhere, though.   It
is strange that Annabelle does not recognise you.
Sometimes I think we have lived together so long
here that she may have lost her memory.   I am
glad you fetched the doctor, William.   Annabelle
will know now her mistake."

There was the sound of footsteps descending the stairs. The doctor entered. He took Goade by the arm and led him on one side.

"You were quite right," he said gravely. "The man upstairs is a poor travelling tinker who has been missing for over a week. I should think that he has been dead at least four days. One of us must stay here whilst the other goes to the police station."

Goade caught feverishly at his hat.

"I will go to the police station," he declared.

III

At last Nicholas Goade was happily situated. He had escaped altogether from the atmosphere of tragedy and gloom, and sat upon his camp stool painting contentedly upon the common adjoining a picturesque village in mid-Devonshire, whose whitewashed cottages, with their fragrant, colour-splashed gardens, snug homesteads and ample population of pleasant-voiced, apple-cheeked maidens, matrons, and kindly-mannered seniors, all betokened an ease of living and happy day-by-day life soothing to the senses and restful to the nerves. It was a land of green meadows, trout streams, and peace, where nobody seemed to have anything to do and plenty of time to do it in. Flip was seated upon her haunches by his side, snapping at flies, and an elderly gentleman, leaning upon a stick, watched his work with puckered lips and a frown upon his forehead.

"Fond of this sort of thing, sir?" Goade presently asked his uninvited companion.

"Not the way you're doing it," was the frank reply.

Goade swung round upon his camp stool at this unexpected criticism.   He saw a rather under-sized, elderly gentleman, neatly dressed in country clothes, with sensitive features and a not unkindly mouth — a man apparently of about sixty years of age.   Accustomed to classifying people on sight, Goade would have put him down as a retired pro-fessional man.

"You don't like my little effort?" he queried.

"I think it's horrible," was the prompt response. "I have been standing here wondering why a grown man like you — a man with a not unintelligent face — should waste his time in such a fashion."

Goade looked dubiously at the awful daub which he had perpetrated, and back again at his critic.

"But I like doing it," he confided.   "It amuses me."

"If it amuses you that's a different matter," the elderly gentleman admitted, leaning a little more heavily upon his stick.   "You may thank your stars you don't have to do it for a living, I am not a gambler, but I would wager that you have never sold one of your productions in your life."

"You are quite right," Goade acquiesced.   "I keep them to decorate my studio."

The little gentleman shivered.

"What a nightmare of a place it must be," he commented.

Half-past twelve sounded from the church clock

on the other side of the common.   Goade covered
up the canvas and prepared for departure.

"In my time," he acknowledged, "I have become
hardened to criticism.   My work, as a matter of
fact, does not find favour with every one.   At the
same time, if I may be permitted to say so, I have
never yet met a stranger who has expressed himself
quite so forcibly."

"Then you've been lucky," was the dry retort.
"I am something of an artist myself, and I assure
you that it is a positive pain to me to contemplate
murderous efforts like yours.   I abhor all forms
of ugliness.   I look upon the man who brings into
the world of actual things a daub, such as you have
just become responsible for, as a criminal —
nothing less than a criminal."

"You depress me exceedingly," Goade sighed.
"Nevertheless," he went on, casting another and
more searching glance at his new friend, "I am
quite sure that your frankness is not meant to be
offensive.   I am now on my way back to the inn.
Do me the favour of drinking a glass of sherry with
me."

The old gentleman gripped his stick firmly and
prepared to accompany his companion.

"On condition," he said, "that you assure me
upon your word of honour that not a penny of
such income as you may be in enjoyment of comes
from dealing in any fashion with your outrageous

work, I will accept your hospitality with pleasure."

"I can offer you that assurance with a clear conscience," Goade told him.

They strolled across the common side by side, conversing indifferently upon general topics. The little old gentleman was interested in his companion; and to a less extent Goade reciprocated the sentiment.

"Living in a small neighbourhood," the former said, "one develops a vein of curiosity as to strangers with whom one is brought into contact. I have lived here for twenty-seven years, and I have become as local as the geese, the postmistress, and the vicar. I am curious about you, sir. What might your profession be?"

"Just at present," Goade confided, "I am resting. I have come into quite a considerable sum of money from a certain enterprise with which I was connected, and I am endeavouring to take a holiday."

"I see," the old gentleman murmured. "And your name?"

"Nicholas Goade."

"Mine is Stanley Witt — Mr. Stanley Witt. I am a retired dealer in curios, second-hand books, ivories, bronzes, and jewellery. Was this enterprise of which you speak a commercial one?"

Goade reflected for a moment. The tracking down through twelve weary months of Ned Bullivant, the greatest criminal New York had ever turned loose upon the world, could scarcely come under such a heading.

"Not exactly," he admitted. "I scarcely know what you would call it. The sort of thing that comes to a man once in a lifetime."

They entered the low portals of the Chidford Arms, descended a step, and turned towards the comfortable bar parlour. Mr. Witt laid his hand upon his companion's arm.

"For God's sake don't bring that truck inside," he begged. "Some one might ask to look at your work, and another glance at it before I have lunched would ruin my appetite."

Goade unburdened himself and laid his easel and canvas against the wall.

"If you go on like this," he grumbled goodnaturedly, "I shall begin to lose confidence in myself."

"The sooner the better," was the eager response. "I think you said that you were on a motor tour. Try fishing. You'll find a stream anywhere round here. Fishing is a reasonable hobby. Better even a bag of golf clubs strapped on behind than that horrible paraphernalia of yours."

They entered the inn parlour, fairly full at that hour of the morning. Goade was greeted with the reserved cordiality accorded to strangers, whilst Mr. Witt, on the other hand, was welcomed enthusiastically. The former, standing a little apart, was able to gauge to a nicety his companion's social position by the nature of the salutations he received. The butcher, the manager from the grocer's shop, and the saddler were cordial but respectful; the doctor, the bank manager, and a prosperous-looking farmer greeted him with friendly equality. Obviously he had established himself as the humorist of the place and an original. More than once his sallies produced little peals of laughter. When, after having returned the compliment of the glass of sherry, he took his leave, most of the others followed him.

"If you've ten minutes to spare before you go away," were his parting words to Nicholas Goade, "and if you really want to know something about the great art of painting, call round at my little house, and I'll show you a landscape which should make you want to destroy every atrocity you have ever perpetrated. Any evening — any time after seven."

"I'll look in with pleasure," Goade promised. . . .

Mr. Witt had scarcely reached the street before he became the subject of conversation amongst the diminished company left behind in the bar parlour.

"It do seem a wonderful thing and a great pleasure," the landlady declared, "to see him almost himself again. It's the first time for a week he's crossed the threshold, and him the most regular of all my customers."

"It was ordained always that he should take his glass of sherry at quarter-past twelve," a farmer remarked.

"Has Mr. Witt been ill?" Goade enquired.

The farmer shook his head; the landlady sighed; the saddler and harness maker in the corner looked gloomily upon the floor. They all hesitated.

"He do seem to have met with trouble, has Mr. Witt," the landlady confided, turning away as she spoke, with the air of one who has finished the subject.

There was a mystery about Mr. Witt — that Goade gathered easily enough during the next few days, from the landlady and the little crowd of bar loungers who were only too ready to discuss him — but what that mystery might be no one seemed to know. A little more than a fortnight previously he had apparently met with trouble of some undefined sort, and now, without warning or explanation, he was subject to fits of isolation, during which no one saw or heard anything of him. There were rumours of cases full of his most precious possessions being sent away by rail to Exeter, and even to London. At such moments as the conversation touched, however vaguely, upon financial matters, the bank manager, whose lips were sealed

by etiquette, retired from the conversation into a
gloomy and portentous silence.   In the end Goade
became interested.   He found himself speculating
often as to the cause of Mr. Witt's trouble, to see
looming up before him the shadow of that crime in
the detection of which he had first won his spurs —
the crime of blackmail.   He would have made an
attempt to gain the little man's confidence, but day
after day passed without a further visit from him.
Finally, after dinner one night at the Chidford
Arms — a dinner of roast veal and bacon, rasp-
berry tart, and Stilton cheese — Flip and her master, equally satisfied with their fare, made their
way up the village street and climbed the hill
towards the few private residences upon its crest,
the second of which had been pointed out to him
as the abode of Mr. Witt.   For five days now the
latter had been invisible, and, curiously enough,
Goade himself, as well as the habitués of the Chidford Arms, had missed the little man's genial presence, his caustic remarks, his humorous sallies.
He had apparently gone into retreat, and any reference to him or to his affairs had been met with
blank silence.   Even Goade, whose sensibilities in
such matters had become blunted, felt guilty almost of intrusion as he rang the shining doorbell.
For several moments nothing happened.   Then a
trim little maidservant of tender years opened the
door and peered out.

"I should like to see Mr. Witt," Goade announced.

The maidservant looked doubtful.

"I don't think he'll see 'e, sir," she replied. "He's none too grand, isn't Mr. Witt — and he's busy."

"You might enquire," Goade persisted. "He asked me to come. I won't keep him long."

The little maidservant departed reluctantly, leaving Goade in a small but cosily furnished hall, redeemed from mediocrity by a wonderful Georgian grandfather's clock and a Chippendale table upon which was a rose bowl of Nankin china. She was absent two or three minutes, at the end of which a door on the ground floor suddenly opened and Mr. Witt looked out. He was collarless and his clothes were dusty. He carried in his hand a hammer.

"What do you want?" he asked sharply.

"I called to have a look at your picture," Goade explained. "If you remember, you offered to show it to me. I've been a little discouraged with my own work the last few days."

"Discouraged! I should think so," was the acid rejoinder. "I can't show you my picture to-night. I'm too busy. Come again in a week or so."

"But, my dear sir," Goade protested, "I sha'n't be here in a week or so. I'm just a tourist. I may move on to-morrow or the next day."

"And paint more pictures?" Mr. Witt enquired, with a shudder.

"And paint more pictures," Goade acquiesced. "I have finished quite a good one with the church tower in the distance, and the geese on the common. Wonderful foreground the geese make! I thought of going south and trying to get the colouring of the moors."

Mr. Witt shivered.

"Come in!" he invited abruptly, standing away from the door.

Goade accepted the invitation and entered an unexpectedly large and pleasant-looking apartment in a state of great disorder. There were two packing cases upon the floor, one of which was half filled with books and a number of statuettes carefully wrapped up in paper. There were empty spaces upon the walls, in the bookcases, and upon the brackets. Mr. Witt took his visitor by the arm and led him to a small canvas hanging in a recess — a landscape deep and rich in colouring.

"That's the real thing," he pointed out. "I don't suppose it's much use talking to you about it. I should think you know about as much of art as my little maid-of-all-work. Consider for a moment that grouping and perspective. If you were to attempt to paint cows that size you'd have them travelling out of the canvas. Look at the beauty of the colouring, too, the slant of that rain on the horizon, so faint one might call it no more than a suggestion, and yet if you analyse it, there it all is. I daresay you don't appreciate it, but, if you looked at it long enough and often enough, you'd probably end by throwing your palette away."

"I know enough to realise that it is a very wonderful picture," Goade admitted. "You have other interesting things too. That, for instance, is a beautiful bronze."

"It ought to be," Mr. Witt acknowledged. "I gave ninety pounds for it as a dealer at the Exford sale."

"And you are now parting with it," Goade remarked, glancing at the half-empty case, and taking his courage into both hands. "Why?"

"That is my business," was the curt reply.

Uninvited, Goade sank into an easy-chair.

"Can I stay for quarter of an hour?" he asked. "I should like to smoke a cigarette with you, if I may?"

"I am expecting a visitor," Mr. Witt said dubiously.

"My staying need not interfere with him. When he comes I will go."

"But I don't want you here when he comes."

Goade showed no signs of moving.

"Mr. Witt," he said, "on our first meeting you indulged in very plain speaking with me. I wasn't annoyed, but I am going to take the liberty of adopting the same tactics with you. Why are you selling off all your belongings like this? Why do you have these periodical fits of behaving like a frightened criminal? Why do you keep a pile of newspapers by your side dealing with the Frangford Murder Case? And who is this young man you are harbouring in the house?"

"Of all the impertinence ——!" Mr. Witt began.

"Nothing of the sort," Goade interrupted — "friendly interest — nothing more or less than that. If I didn't believe that I could help you, I shouldn't have said a word."

"How the devil can you or any one else help me?" Mr. Witt groaned.

Goade settled himself a little more comfortably in his chair.

"I'll see about that when you've told me the whole story," he replied.

Mr. Witt glanced helplessly around. His visitor looked the personification of strength and self-reliance as he lounged in his chair, and for the first time the little man ached for a confidant. He pointed towards the pile of newspapers.

"Have you read the Frangford Murder Case?" he asked.

"Every line," Goade admitted. "Rather a hobby of mine, these cases."

"You know that the cashier of the Frangford Bank was murdered, and two of the bank clerks

from the main office who were due to take their holiday on the following day have not been heard of?"

"Quite so," Goade agreed. "The names of the
two young men are Stephen Hannaford and — by
Jove!"

Mr. Witt nodded shortly.

"John Eardley-Witt was the name of the other
one," he said. "The 'Eardley' wraps it up a little
— an uncle on his mother's side left him a small
sum of money and the name — but John Eardley-
Witt is my son."

"You are sure that they are definitely suspected?" Goade asked. "The newspapers seem to
be very vague about the matter."

"You are, I suppose, the sort of fellow who can
keep his mouth shut?" Mr. Witt demanded.

"I have the reputation of being a safe confidant,"
Goade declared.

"Very well then," the other went on. "My son
is lying in Plymouth, waiting for a chance to get
away to South America. Hannaford is upstairs
at the present moment. That's as much as they
have had of their holiday."

"The young man I saw with the pale face peering out from behind the curtains?" Goade asked.

Mr. Witt stared at him.

"Either you must have damned good eyes or the
young fellow's a bigger fool than I thought he
was," he remarked sharply.

"I have the knack of observation," Goade admitted. "I picked it up early in life. It goes with my profession."

"What is your profession?" Mr. Witt enquired. "Not that it matters what the devil you call yourself, so long as you don't call yourself an artist."

"Then we'll let my profession alone for the minute," Goade decided. "Now, get on with the story. What's young Hannaford doing here?"

"He's come for money. He's been twice before."

"What do they want money for? If they committed the murder, they got away with fifteen hundred pounds."

"They daren't use it," Mr. Witt confided. "It was all in Bank of England notes."

"How much have you parted with altogether?" Goade enquired.

"I have sold nearly a thousand pounds' worth of my belongings," Mr. Witt confessed, with a little groan. "My picture will have to go now."

"I shouldn't let it," Goade advised. "What have you done — sold the things outright?"

"Pawned them," was the bitter reply.

"Keep the tickets carefully. You never can tell what may happen. Let me talk to that young man upstairs."

"What on earth would be the use of that? You'd only frighten him to death."

"I'd like to hear his story."

"I've heard it once," Mr. Witt groaned. "I don't want to hear it again. Besides, what's the good?"

"Look here," Goade begged, "fetch him down. Let him think I'm an old friend of the family. Things can't seem any worse to you than they do now, can they? Well, give me a chance!"

"I don't think he'll come," Mr. Witt said doubtfully. "He's terrified if the doorbell rings."

"We'll go to him then," Goade insisted, rising.

Eventually, after a little more persuasion on the latter's part, they did so. Mr. Witt led the way upstairs, and opened the door of a pleasantly furnished bedroom. Its occupant was sprawling in an easy-chair, with his feet upon another, smoking a cigarette, a half-empty tumbler by his side and a decanter and syphon upon the dressing table. The windows were closed, and the room was fetid with tobacco smoke. The young man — a thin, pale youth with a bad complexion and weedy figure — sprang to his feet and cowered back as he realised the presence of a stranger. He wore a blue serge suit badly out of shape and in need of brushing. He had kicked off his shoes and was sitting in his socks. His linen was not irreproachable.

"Who's this, Mr. Witt?" he demanded. "Who've you brought here?"

"An old friend, Stephen," Mr. Witt replied. "He's all right. He's not giving anything away."

"What does he want, then?" the young man continued peevishly.

Goade seated himself on the edge of the bed.

"I thought I'd like to ask you a few questions if you didn't mind," he suggested. "I might be able to help you."

"What sort of questions?"

"About the case," Goade answered bluntly. "What made you do it?"

The young man puffed viciously at his cigarette.

"John and I were always hard up," he explained. "These banks starve us, and then expect us to live and dress like gentlemen. I was in debt; so was John. They were bound to find it out sooner or later, and then we should have had to go. We were both out at the Frangford Branch for two months last winter. We couldn't help seeing how easy it would be. We talked about it until the idea grew on us. We couldn't think about anything else. Harrigan, the man over there, was all alone, and the day we made up our minds we knew he must have at least fifteen hundred pounds. There are some big factories near, with pay-day on Friday afternoon. Well, we just did it. That's all."

"Robbery is one thing," Goade observed. "Murder is another."

"I swear we never meant to shoot him," the young man declared, gripping the side of the chair.

"Neither of us had ever handled a revolver before in our lives. We only meant to frighten him. I can swear that. John can swear it. The beastly thing went off."

"Who was holding it at the time?" Goade asked.

The young man was suddenly silent.

"We've both sworn," he said, "never to tell that."

"Why do you want all this money from Mr. Witt?" Goade continued. "The passages won't cost much."

"We've had to pay several hundred pounds to a man who saw us near Frangford," Hannaford groaned. "He's got to know where John is, and he's soaking us all the time. It's costing a hell of a lot too, for John to lie low. It's a snug place, but they've got an idea we're in trouble, and they charge like the devil. With any luck, though, we'll be off next week to South America."

"Have you ever been in trouble before?"

"No," the young man snapped. "I don't know who you are, but I don't like your questions. Take him away, please, Mr. Witt. It's bad enough hanging round here while you raise the money, without having strangers coming in to frighten one."

Goade rose to his feet.

"Well, it's a bad job," he admitted. "I'm afraid there's nothing any one can do to help either of you."

"Of course there isn't," was the irritable rejoinder. "The money's what we want, the money as quick as it can be got hold of. And don't run out of whisky, Mr. Witt. My nerves are something terrible, especially in the night. The rest of that bottle won't last long."

The two men descended the stairs in silence. Mr. Witt had lost all his peppery manner. The gleam had gone from his eyes, his mouth had weakened, was almost inclined to tremble. Goade laid his hand protectively upon his shoulder.

"Look here, my friend," he said, "there doesn't seem much to be done, but I wouldn't give up hope. I shall be away to-morrow all day — got to run up to Barnstable. When do you expect to get the money for the things you're sending off now?"

"Not until Thursday morning at the earliest," Mr. Witt replied.

"Very well, then. Don't part with your young man before then. Keep him here until I come back."

Mr. Witt looked up quickly.

"Anything in your mind?"

"Nothing definite — just an idea. The great thing is not to part with the young man until I am back on Thursday."

"No fear of that," Mr. Witt sighed. "I can't get the cheque before then, and afterwards I'll have to go to the bank and cash it."

"Has your son written you himself at all?"
Mr. Witt shook his head.

"It wouldn't be safe," he answered, with a groan.
"It's a small place this, and they'd even know his
handwriting at the post-office."

"I had forgotten that," Goade admitted thoughtfully. "Until Thursday then."

Thursday was a morning of disappointment for
Mr. Witt. The post brought neither the cheque
from Exeter which he was expecting nor any message from his new friend, to whose return he had
been looking forward with a faint, scarcely acknowledged hope of help. His breakfast was
barely finished when there came a stamping on the
ceiling. With a little shudder, he ascended to
meet his unwelcome guest. Stephen Hannaford,
in his night attire — he had just apparently scrambled out of bed — was even more unprepossessing
than in the daytime. His eyes were terribly blood-
shot, and his hands were shaking.

"Have you got the cheque?" he demanded.

"It hasn't come," Mr. Witt admitted.

The young man's language was such that his
host covered his ears with his hands.

"You want your son to swing, do you, and me
too?" the infuriated youth exclaimed. "Look
here," he went on, "a promise is a promise, but if it
comes to saving my neck I'll tell you something.

It wasn't I who carried the revolver.   I can prove
that.   It was your son who'll have to swing, not me.
I may get a lifer, but he'll go to the scaffold."

Mr. Witt closed his eyes for a moment.   The
strain of the last few days had been great, and he
was feeling giddy.

"I sent away everything I possessed of value,"
he announced in a dull tone.   "I begged that the
cheque should be posted yesterday.   It will certainly come by the second post."

"What time's that?"

"Three o'clock."

"In time to get notes from the bank?"

"In plenty of time."

The young man crawled back into bed.

"Send me up some more tea," he directed, "and
I want two more tins of Gold Flake cigarettes.
Tell that tweeny of yours to look alive."

Mr. Witt turned towards the door and did the
bidding of his unpleasant visitor.   Afterwards he
locked himself into his own room.   In his way he
was a proud man, and he had reached the limits of
his endurance.   No one ever knew — he scarcely
remembered himself — how he spent the morning.
There was a pretence of lunch, a restless pacing of
the room, the postman's arrival, the expected letter, and a cheque for nine hundred pounds.

"How much is it?" Hannaford called over the
banisters.

"Nine hundred pounds."

"Leg it down to the bank then, quick," the young man enjoined eagerly. "Call at the garage coming back and order the car to take me to Plymouth. There's a moon to-night, and I'll get there by four o'clock."

Mr. Witt brushed himself mechanically, put on his hat, picked up his gloves and stick, and made his way, silent and ghostlike, through the streets of the little market town. He was scarcely conscious of the greetings he received, of the sympathetic glances his appearance provoked. He wrote out an open cheque and handed it across the counter, together with his credit, stated his wishes in brief words, and buttoned up the pile of notes in his breast pocket. Then he turned to climb the hill again homewards. He was brought to a standstill by the noisy clatter of an ancient Ford car and the yapping of a small white dog. Mr. Goade, looking a little tired, drew up at the side of the path.

"Young man still with you?" he asked.

"He is still there," Mr. Witt acknowledged. "I've just got the money for him. He's going this afternoon."

"Is he?" Goade murmured under his breath. "Well, get in, Mr. Witt. I'll drive you home."

Mr. Witt mounted the car in silence. His half-wistful glance of enquiry towards Goade elicited no response.   After all, what could Goade or any man do?

"I've got to call at a garage," Mr. Witt announced.

"What for?"

"For a car to take the young man down to Plymouth.   He hopes they'll get off on Saturday now.   They've got their berths all right, if they can stop this other fellow's mouth."

"We'll see about the car presently," Goade said. "There's just one word I want to have with your young friend first."

"He's in a nasty temper," Mr. Witt groaned.

"I'll humour him all right," Goade promised.

He pulled up outside the gate and followed his companion into the house.   The young man was waiting at the top of the staircase.

"Have you brought the money?" he demanded. "Where's the car?"

"I have the money," Mr. Witt assured him. "The car will be here presently.   Mr. Goade wants one word with you."

"Blast Mr. Goade!" the young man exclaimed angrily.   "I've no time for fooling about with any one.   You ought to know that."

"I sha'n't keep you a moment," Goade promised, with spurious good humour.   "Come along down to the sitting room."

Hannaford descended the stairs with sullen re-

luctance.   Goade waited until he was well inside
the room.   Then, with his back to the door, he advanced towards the chair into which the young man
had thrown himself.

"Hold out your hands," he ordered.

"What the hell for?"

"For these," Goade replied, drawing a pair of
handcuffs from his pocket.

Hannaford made a dash for the door, but he was
as pulp in his captor's grasp.   With one hand
Goade held his wrists together, then pushed him
back into his chair.

"Stay there!" he directed.

"Who are you?" the young man spluttered.
"What are you doing with those things?"

"I'm a detective officer — pretty well known at
Scotland Yard," Goade acknowledged.   "I'm supposed to be down here on a holiday, but I'm never
above doing a stroke of work when necessary."

"You're betraying my trust," Mr. Witt cried
bitterly.   "You accepted my confidence.   You
gave me your word."

Goade led him to a chair.

"You sit down, my friend," he enjoined, "and
don't you worry.   I put the handcuffs on him to
keep him quiet, but the only charge I've got against
him is of obtaining money under false pretences.
When we've got the money back, we'll decide how
to deal with him later."

"But the bank robbery?" Mr. Witt exclaimed.

Goade laughed scornfully.

"I don't know anything about your son, Mr. Witt," he said — "I shall know more about him presently — but as regards this young man, he hasn't got the pluck to steal an old lady's reticule. The man who robbed the bank and shot the cashier will be arrested this afternoon, and I can assure you he's a very different type of person from this."

There was a moist gleam in Mr. Witt's eyes, and he was trembling violently. Goade patted him soothingly upon the shoulder.

"Look here, Mr. Witt," he explained, "it's really quite a simple matter. Your son's holiday and this young man's commenced the day after the murder and robbery. This was simply a coincidence. They may have started off to spend a portion of it together; that I don't know. One newspaper only spoke of two clerks being missing — a statement which was afterwards contradicted. This young man Hannaford thought out a very ingenious scheme. He brought you the newspaper in case you hadn't seen it, and, as I gather, confessed that he and your son had committed the robbery and shot the cashier. They have neither of them done anything of the sort. Your son, from all I can hear, is a young man in excellent repute. Our friend who is wearing those handcuffs so gracefully had been given notice by the manager to leave

at the expiration of his holiday.   Now, are you
getting hold of things, Mr. Witt?   It seems sim-
pler every moment, eh?"

"Oh, it's simple enough," Hannaford muttered.
"If you hadn't come blundering along, it would
have worked out all right too."

"It might have," Goade admitted.   "Yours
wasn't a bad scheme," he continued, "but what
should you have done if Mr. Witt's son had written
to his father about his holiday or anything, or come
down here?"

"I sent a telegram in Mr. Witt's name from a
village near here," the young man confessed surlily.
"I told him that his father had gone on a fortnight's
motoring tour with a friend and would meet him
at the Grand Hotel, Llandudno."

"Capital!" Goade approved.   "Very ingenious
indeed!   And now what about the rest of that
money?"

"I've spent it."

"I think not.   A little inconvenient for you, perhaps, but allow me to search."

Resistance was hopeless.   Goade thrust his hand
into the pocket of the young man's coat and drew
out a packet of notes, which he laid upon the table.

"All there?" he asked.

"All except ten pounds."

Mr. Witt's elbows were upon the table.   He was
leaning forward, and his face was hidden in his
hands.   Goade patted him on the back.

"Now, what shall we do with this young man," he asked. "He deserves — well, God knows what he deserves! The 'cat' would be my idea, but I'll leave it to you. I'm the law, but I'm the law on a holiday. You've got practically all your money back. You've got the pawn tickets to re-collect your treasures. Nothing will ever recompense you for the days of suffering you must have had. You can get him twelve months' imprisonment, if that's any satisfaction, or you can throw him out of the house."

Mr. Witt stood up. He was already looking better. Some of the lines upon his face had gone, but there was a mistiness about his eyes which changed his whole expression.

"I don't want to prosecute him," he said. "Send him away. I hate the sight of him."

The young man stood up, and Goade, with an expert touch, relieved him of the handcuffs. Then, with his hand upon his collar, he marched him out of the room, marched him to the front door, and, picking him up, sent him sprawling through the rose bushes.

"So that's that!" he remarked, looking in through the window at Mr. Witt. "You'll like to be alone for an hour or so?"

"It's true? It's all true?" the little man insisted.

"Of course it is," Goade assured him. "You know I'm used to hearing stories and confessions, and I knew there was something wrong about that young man's tale. I've been to Bristol and had an hour's talk on the telephone with Scotland Yard since I saw you. They speak very highly of your son at the bank. By the by, I'm expecting you to bring him to dinner to-night at the inn. He'll be here within an hour or so. Half-past seven. Don't trouble to change. I haven't those sort of clothes myself. . . . That's all right!"

Goade hurried off, started up the Ford, and drove down to the inn.

"This is all very well, Miss Flip," he confided, "but it's beginning to be a sort of 'busman's holiday' for me."

At half-past seven Mr. Witt, his old self, bright-eyed and happy, came into the bar parlour, accompanied by a tall, sunburnt young man whom he introduced to Goade as his son. He was carrying a brown-paper parcel under his arm, which for a moment, however, he ignored. The bar parlour was full, and there was a little chorus of acclamation as its occupants realised the change in their very popular neighbour. Every one was anxious, too, to shake hands with his son.

"Gentlemen," Mr. Witt invited, "give your orders, please. I want you all to take a glass of wine with me and drink to the health of my friend here — Mr. Nicholas Goade. He's the worst painter in the world, but the best of fellows, and he has just done me a very great service."

There was more acclamation, a quarter of an hour or so of good fellowship, and afterwards Goade led the way to the table in the coffee room which was laid for dinner. There was a gold-foiled bottle in an ice pail, and another in reserve. Mr. Witt reverently undid the strings of the parcel which he had been carrying.

"Mr. Goade," he said, "I am taking the liberty of bringing you a small present. If it has the effect upon your taste I imagine it may have, you will perhaps change your hobby."

Mr. Goade accepted the picture with a little word of protest. It was a very beautiful picture, though, and the more he looked at it, the more he realised the things which had been in its donor's mind.

"And in return," Mr. Witt concluded, as they seated themselves at the table, "I am going to ask you to give me that little canvas I saw you working on the first time we met — the one with the church behind and the geese in the foreground."

"It's a damned bad picture," Goade acknowledged a little ruefully, "but you shall have it."

"It's a damn bad picture," Mr. Witt agreed fervently, "but I want it."

IV

A WEST wind travelling fitfully over the count-
less rabbit holes on Martinhoe Common brought
little whiffs of a familiar and entrancing odour to
Flip's twitching nostrils. She opened one eye and
then the other, rose from her seat in the Ford car
which was grinding its way up a steep ascent, and
with her forepaws upon the side, looked longingly
out. Goade, having completed the ascent, brought
the car to a standstill by the side of the road and
drew a packet of letters which he had just collected
at the village post-office from his pocket. He
opened the door of the car.

"Go and enjoy yourself, Flip," he enjoined.
"We will rest for quarter of an hour."

Flip, a quivering, fat ball of excitement, leaped
into the road and darted towards the arena of the
most elusive sport which ever brought joy to the
heart of a Sealyham. Goade read his letters one
by one and stuffed them into his pocket. The last
— enclosed in a heavy cream envelope with the
black initials "S. Y." on the back — he opened with
more interest than the others. It was from his
Chief, a few lines, short but to the point:

MY DEAR GOADE, — Glad to hear you are getting so much amusement out of your holiday. Without the least desire to interfere in any way with your artistic efforts, I should like to suggest that if you pass through the small market-town of Bodstaple you call and see the local sergeant there. It appears that a number of quite inexplicable accidents have taken place in the vicinity for which the local police are absolutely unable to account. Faulkener, the Chief Constable of the county, whom I think you know, has been over from Exeter, and I understand that if they don't come to some conclusion shortly they are going to appeal to us. I'm not asking you to take this on professionally in any way, but I thought it might amuse you to study the matter if you should be in the neighbourhood.

Goade replaced the letter in its envelope and buttoned it up in his breast coat pocket. Afterwards he studied the map for a moment, filled his pipe, and leaned back to enjoy the soft summer sunshine. The place brought reminiscences of odours other than that which had moved Flip to ecstasy; suggestions of wild thyme, the faint almond-like scent of the gorse, an occasional waft of sweetness from the drooping honeysuckle in a clump of bushes a short distance away. It was a morning for lazy and sensuous idleness, a morning when even to have taken out his easel would have seemed too hard a task.   Goade leaned back in his car with his hands clasped behind his head and gave himself up to most unprofessional meditation.   The most adroit criminal in the world would have found it difficult to awaken him from his lethargy at that moment.   The sport of man-hunting had lost its appeal.   What a country this to end one's days in, if only the sun would shine more often!

A sharp bark in the road brought him back to the present.   He looked over the side of the car. Flip, the most disreputable specimen of canine existence the mind of man could conceive, climbed on to the step and waited for the door to open. Each one of her short legs was caked in soil.   Her stomach was black from investigations in a peat bog.   Her nose and mouth, up to her eyes, were indistinguishable.   She wagged her tail a little self-consciously and jumped up to her place.

"Into the next pond you go, old lady," Goade muttered — a threat which left her entirely unmoved.

They jogged on through the picturesque country — master and dog — until they reached the pleasant, straggling village of Bodstaple, a village which seemed to extend the whole length of one side of a steep combe.   There was a trout stream down below, winding its way through a strip of rich green meadowland, and above, one clean white street, widening to a little square around which were the principal houses and shops. Goade drew up at the homely looking inn, ordered lunch, and strolled over to the police station opposite — a flower-covered abode with irregular blocks of white pavement leading through a garden riotous in colour. Sergeant Elworthy was at home and apparently off duty. He wore his official trousers, a grey shirt, and very little else.

"I am on a holiday," Goade explained, after he had presented his card, "and I don't wish to interfere unless I can be of service. The Chief, however, has written me from Scotland Yard that you are rather troubled about some accidents here. He doesn't give me any particulars. I don't know whether you would care to confide in me."

The sergeant, a large and ponderous man, examined the card, holding it between his thumb and forefinger. He spelled the name out to himself.

"Goade," he reflected. "It was an Inspector Goade took the big reward from America."

"I was the lucky person," his visitor confessed.

The sergeant looked reverently across at him.

"You're mighty welcome, Mr. Goade," he said. "It may seem a small affair this to a brain like yours, but it do get us local people fairly flummoxed."

"Tell me about it," Goade invited, filling his pipe and passing his pouch across.

The sergeant was a very deliberate man and it took him five minutes to follow his companion's example and get started. Goade was careful not to hurry him. He had developed a theory that you got the most out of people by permitting them to use their own methods.

"It begun four months ago," the sergeant explained, "with young Ned Spurrell, the Squire's underkeeper, a harmless young fellow enough, though he do be fond of a drop of cider. He were walking through the wood late one night on his beat when he had the sudden feeling — to use his own words — that 'summat was biting into his flesh.' He went toppling over and when he came to an hour or so later there was a wound in his leg that ain't healed yet."

"What sort of a wound?" Goade asked curiously.

"A nasty, jagged place as though some one had hit him with an iron implement. He's been on his back for six weeks and powerful sorry for himself he be. Then, while he do lie there, pretty well the same thing happens to John Strone. He be a farm labourer up at the Hall Farm, and he were walking home from the inn one night — a trifle merry but nothing to hurt — and he suddenly felt that something had gripped him by the leg. Over he toppled and when he come to his trouser were all torn and he were in pretty much the same state as Ned. What do you make of that, Mr. Goade?"

Goade shook his head.

"I'm afraid I can't make anything out of it yet," he admitted. "I should like to hear the doctor's account of the wound."

"That you may have at any moment," the sergeant replied, "for Doctor Graves he do live in the village and he'll be home from his rounds before one. A fair puzzled man the doctor, too. After Strone there did come a youngster what hadn't been in these parts long — Michael Kerrison — a loose-living lad, I'm afraid. He were on his way — some says to do a bit of poaching — one dark night, and all of a sudden he felt a bang on the back of his head as though he had been hit by a great piece of board, and over he went. He never heerd a footstep or see'd a soul. It were just as though a ton of wood had fallen from the skies and knocked him silly. Last of all — a fortnight ago come Thursday — Mr. Emmett, the grocer, was out after an evening rabbit, on Farmer Jobson's meadow, where he'd a perfect right to be, and crossing the stepping stones the same thing happened to he as had happened to Strone and Kerrison and Spurrell. When he come to he'd the same nature wound in his leg, but he was lying on the bank and he will have it that some one had pulled him out fearing like that he might be drowned, and left him there."

"None of these men were robbed or interfered with in any way?" Goade asked.

"Not a thing touched.   Most of 'em had money in their pockets, and there it was.   Mr. Emmett, he'd five pounds in treasury notes and some loose silver.   It was there to the last penny."

"They were all of different families?   Nothing to connect them at all?"

"Not a thing.   The lad was almost a stranger to the others.   Spurrell and Strone were just friendly like, but not intimate."

"Any bad characters in the village?"

"There isn't a living soul," was the emphatic reply, "as one'd suspect of a dirty deed.   There's little trouble here for the police and less now than ever since the Welsh revivalists came along.   They do seem in their way to have done a power of good, although not saying that such was necessary in these parts.   We bean't such sinful folks as in the towns."

"Have you any theories?"

"There isn't one a sane man could keep in his head like," the sergeant declared.

"Suspect any one?"

"There bean't a soul in the place one could suspect."

"No strangers about?"

"Not a sign of one."

Goade rose to his feet.

"Well, no wonder you're puzzled, Sergeant," he said.   "I'll have a talk with the doctor during the afternoon, and maybe one of the men who met with the accident.   When do you go on duty again?"

"At ten o'clock to-night, sir," the man replied. "There's naught but simple jobs in the daytime here.   I've taken to prowling about in the darkness on the chance of finding something."

"I'll be in before then," Goade promised, and took his leave.

He visited the doctor after an excellent luncheon — a cheerful old gentleman who had absolutely no enlightenment to offer.

"All I can tell you," he confided, "is that each of these three men met with his accident or whatever it was in about the same place — halfway up the shin bone.   It just looks as though some one had struck them a savage blow with a jagged metal weapon of some sort, ripped the flesh up and just bared the bone.   As for Kerrison, what he got was plain enough.   He got a bang on the back of the head with a blunt weapon of considerable breadth. A plank of wood would give you the idea."

"It seems an extraordinary business," Goade observed.

The doctor shrugged his shoulders.   He was a very hard-worked man, and his manner indicated that it was his business to heal wounds and not to worry about how they were received.   He made no attempt to detain his visitor when the latter rose to take his leave, and hastened off to his consulting room.   Goade put his head in at the police station.

"I shall stay the night anyway, Sergeant," he confided; "perhaps two or three days.   Which is the most intelligent of the men who met with an accident to his leg?"

"Ned Spurrell, he do be the most of a scholard," the policeman conceded.   "I'll walk with you so far any time this afternoon."

"About four then," Goade suggested.

Goade, as he pushed open the gate of Ned Spurrell's cottage, paused upon the red-tiled path between two great bushes of sweetbriar, and listened. The casement window of the room on the ground floor was wide open and through it there floated the sound of the most beautiful voice, it seemed to him, that he had ever heard in his life — the voice of a woman reading a chapter from one of the Gospels.   Even as he lingered, the cadence of it died away.   He heard the closing of the book, a momentary silence, and then her voice again, reciting the Lord's Prayer, to which there came in an undertone, a half-shamed, half-earnest echo.   He waited until the last words had left their lips before he knocked at the door.   A moment or so later it was opened.   A girl, wearing a perfectly plain grey dress, made with the severity of a uniform, her hair brushed smoothly back from her beautiful forehead, stood looking out at him.   He knew at once that it was the woman with the wonderful voice. He realised too that, notwithstanding the simplicity of her attire, and slight pallor of complexion, she was probably the most beautiful woman he had ever seen in his life. Her complexion was almost unnaturally clear, her features madonna-like in their purity, her faint smile, even to him, a stranger, the gentlest and sweetest thing in the world.

"I called to see Mr. Spurrell," he explained. "You are probably the nurse. Is he well enough to talk to me?"

"Quite well enough," she answered. "I am not the nurse, but they have left me in charge for a little time. Shall I tell him your name?"

"He wouldn't know it," Goade replied. "All the same I should be glad to see him for a minute or two."

She led the way in and bent over the couch.

"Here is a gentleman to see you," she announced. "Your mother will be back now in a quarter of an hour. I shall leave you with him."

"You'll come to-morrow," the young man begged.

"I shall come to-morrow," she acquiesced, almost under her breath. "I shall come every day until you promise."

His eyes followed her to the door, which Goade held open for her. She looked around and smiled.

"May God have you in His keeping," she said, as she passed out.

Goade closed the door and came over to the bed.

"So you're Ned Spurrell," he began, drawing a chair up to the man's side. "I wish you'd tell me who that very attractive young person is?"

"Her name is Mary Tennent," was the somewhat diffident reply. "She and her brother are after mission work round about here. They've come from Wales."

"I should think all you unmarried lads would easily get converted," Goade remarked, smiling.

The young man declined to take the matter lightly.

"She is marvellous," he confided in an awed tone. "The way she talks about religion, too — there was never a parson like it for making you feel things. Who might you be, sir?"

"I came to see you about the accident," Goade explained. "Queer sort of affair, wasn't it?"

"Are you from the Insurance?" Ned Spurrell asked suspiciously.

"If you really want to know," Goade answered, "although I'd rather you didn't talk about me, I am connected with the police."

The invalid chuckled.

"Connected with the police!" he scoffed. "They be a pretty lot. Four on us done in like this and not even an arrest."

"Well, it's rather an unusual sort of an affair?" Goade pointed out. "Tell me exactly what happened."

"Why *it* happened — that's all; I was walking straight along, harmless as might be, smoking my pipe, and it was just as though summat had hit me an almighty whack on the right shin with a crowbar. I toppled right over, couldn't move or drag my leg an inch, and before I knowed where I was I were a gone 'un."

"You didn't hear any one around?"

"I didn't hear any one, and there wurn't any one. I'd go bail for that," was the dogged reply. "A most mysterious-like business though it was. I've lain here and puzzled about it until my head ached."

"Have you told any one the exact spot where it happened?"

"The sergeant knows to an inch. There ain't anything there to harm a body, leastways so he says. He's been there often enough since."

"I'll get him to show me the place," Goade said. "No one about here with any grudge against you, I suppose, or anything of that sort?"

"Not a soul. Besides, there's the others," the young man pointed out. "There isn't a more popular young chap in the village than John Strone. Shall you be going to see him?"

"Presently. I want to see all four of you who have met with these singular accidents."

"I don't know as it will do you any good," the gamekeeper warned him. "They none of them knows any more about it than I do."

"In our profession," Goade observed, "one stumbles upon a clue in the most unexpected moments."

"You be a detective, I suppose?"

Goade nodded.

"Yes," he admitted, "I belong to Scotland Yard. Just now I'm having a holiday."

"Tell us some stories about burglaring and such-like," the young man proposed. "Its dull lying here now she's paid me her visit."

"Does this young lady revivalist visit all of you?" Goade asked.

"I reckon so," was the somewhat sullen reply. "She went to see Strone twice one day when he were bad."

"What sect does she belong to?"

"None at all.   That's the wonderful part of her and her brother too.   If you're church, she just wants you to feel something inside about church that you've never felt before.   She tries to 'light' something, she says.   If you're chapel it's just the same.   I'm going to church with her the first day I can hobble out."

Goade, after the recital of a few personal experiences, presently found the place where he had left the sergeant to wait for him, and examined the scene of Spurrell's accident.   It was just a rough path, a little overgrown with bracken, and the closest investigation yielded not the slightest explanation of the mystery.

"You'd like to see the other misfortunate young men, Mr. Goade?" the sergeant suggested. "They're none of them so far away."

"I'll see them to-morrow," Goade promised. "Don't let me keep you, Sergeant.   I'm going to smoke a pipe here at the edge of the wood.   If you'll call for me when you make your round to-night I might have a stroll with you."

The man saluted and withdrew.   Goade seated himself on a low bank and awaited Flip's pleasure. Presently he heard a gate opened and closed. Coming across the strip of meadowland towards him was Mary Tennent.   He watched her approach with critical but admiring eyes.   She walked, it seemed to him, as he had never seen another woman walk in his life, and her smile as she recognised him was a bewildering thing.

"You have come to see the place where Mr. Spurrell met with his accident?" she enquired.

He nodded.

"And you," he ventured, "have been to see one of the other sufferers?"

She smiled.

"I am very happy this afternoon," she confided. "Mr. Strone has been so obstinate.   Just now I think the words of a little prayer I said moved him. He has promised to go to chapel with me the first Sunday he is able to get out."

"You'll have your hands full with all these young men," he remarked.

"What do I mind?" she rejoined. "It is my life. It is what I was born for, what I live for. Now, the only one who hasn't promised is Michael Kerrison. He is difficult, but he will promise before I go."

"What made you take up this work?" he asked.

"God put it into my head," she answered simply. "My father preached until the day he died. My brother is something wonderful. I do my best. There are times when I am very successful."

"Don't you find these young men get jealous of one another sometimes?"

She smiled back at him frankly.

"Of course now and then they are foolish," she admitted. "They don't understand of how little account love-making and marrying and those things are compared with eternity. I'd give my poor body to all of them if I could make them feel the great things."

He looked at her curiously. There was no doubt as to her sincerity. The light of a divine mysticism shone from her eyes. One could imagine her a Joan of Arc, welcoming, exulting in sacrifice. Her body — what did it matter? She lived outside.

"Who is with you here?" he enquired a little abruptly. "Didn't I hear something about a brother?"

"I am alone with my brother," she told him. "We have a little caravan. We came all the way from Wales in it. He is a very clever carpenter and tinker, and sometimes I do sewing at ladies' houses. We have no money except what we make by the way, but that is always plenty."

"Do you know," he asked her, "that you are very beautiful?"

"It is the grace of God which is in me," she said quite simply.

His breath was taken away. He knew perfectly well that she was sincere, that every word she said came from her heart.

"Still, I can't help thinking that you must find it more than a little troublesome sometimes with all these young men," he persisted. "Don't some of them want to marry you, for instance?"

She laughed softly.

"Most of them," she admitted. "I would marry them all, if I could. I would marry any one to save his soul."

"Even me?"

She laid her hand upon his without a moment's hesitation — a soft, cool hand, delightful to feel.

"Of course I would," she assured him. "If by marrying you I could make you see the light, could take you up with me to God, of course I would marry you."

"But then," he went on, still holding her hand, "there are Ned Spurrell and Michael Kerrison and John Strone."

"I know," she assented a little sadly. "I shall take them all to church or chapel with me, and they will all want me to marry them. Sometimes when I go away they are angry and they forget all they have promised — but not always. Many of them remember, and if only a few remember it is worth while. . . . What about you? Please tell me your name again."

"Goade — Nicholas Goade."

"What about you, Mr. Nicholas Goade?"

"I don't think I'm irreligious," he said. "I am just one of those persons who can't arrive at any satisfactory solution, I suppose, and who drift."

"It is the most dangerous state of all," she declared, gripping his fingers. "You try, don't you, to solve the future and to understand God with your brain. Men can't do that. It's faith you want — faith. Faith you must have. You must get it at any price. You must pray for it — pray until the words fail you — but you must have it, or think what will happen when you die."

Her voice was quivering with eagerness; the fever was upon her.

"I must come and hear your brother preach," he suggested.

"You shall talk with him," she agreed. "He is wonderful. He has made more converts than any one else. Come and find him now. I will show you where we live."

He rose to his feet and whistled for Flip, who had been engaged upon disappointing investigations around some rabbit holes. The girl took his arm quite naturally.

"I should love you to be one of my brothers," she confided; "my brothers in the Great Faith. If any one can make you see the truth, James can. He has the gift of tongues."

"You too have a gift," he reminded her.

"The gift of Mary Magdalen," she sighed. "She also was beautiful. My beauty, such as it is, is for any one whom it can bring a little nearer to salvation."

They came out from the wood into a meadow by the stream. Two small caravans were drawn up a few yards from the gate. From inside the smaller one came the sound of the whirring of a lathe.

"That is my brother at work," she told him. "James!"

The door presently opened and a young man appeared. Goade studied him appraisingly — a typical visionary, hollow-cheeked, with cavernous eyes, jet black hair, lips moving even in silence.

"Who is this, Mary?" he asked.

"A friend," she answered. "I found him at Ned Spurrell's cottage. He is coming to the meeting to-night. He is still of the Kingdom of the World, James. You will speak to him."

Goade, the least impressionable of men, felt the warmth of the young man's smile, the earnestness of his gaze.

"If words winged with the truth can bring you to the knowledge of it, you shall hear them," he promised.

He locked the door of the little caravan from which he had issued.

"Is that your workshop?" Goade enquired.

The young man nodded, but ignored his questioner's obvious curiosity. He made his way to the larger caravan and busied himself at a bookcase, selecting various volumes. The girl brought her companion to the steps and invited him to enter.

"There is my bed," she pointed out, inclining her head towards a spotlessly neat bunk, by the side of which on a small table stood a bowl of flowers and a Bible. From the open window a soft breeze swept through the place.

"You have chosen a delightful spot for your camping ground," Goade remarked.

"At night it is wonderful," she confided. "I lie here and I can see the stars and I can hear the night birds in the woods. There is an owl's nest in those trees there, and a nightingale just across the stream. Sometimes it is too beautiful to sleep though. Then I get up and walk around."

"It must have been close by here that Ned Spurrell met with his accident," Goade reflected. "You didn't hear him call out or anything?"

"We heard nothing," the girl answered.

Goade took his leave and she walked with him to the top of the field.

"At eight o'clock in the Square," she reminded him.

"I shall be there," he promised.

"I shall pray for you," she whispered. "I think I shall pray as I never prayed before."

She was clinging to his arm quite frankly, and Goade, with all his experience of men and women, was confused, bewildered by her attitude. If she were indeed unconscious of any physical self, she still seemed to retain a most desirable leaven of humanity. One could almost have sworn to a glint of coquetry in her eyes as she bade him farewell, and watched him march off down the road. He turned to wave his hand, and he wondered whether it was his fancy that her fingers touched her lips before they waved their reply. . . .

"Any luck, sir?" the sergeant asked him, as they met in the street.

Goade shook his head.

"I think your little corner of the world, Sergeant," he replied, "is going to set us all guessing."

After dinner he lit a pipe and strolled out to witness what was almost a royal procession, the procession of Mary Tennent with a hymn book in her hand, and her brother with a Bible, passing down the village street. People whom they met clasped both of them by the hand. Many turned around and followed. Before they reached the market place they were the centre of a little escorting group. People streamed from all sides. Willing hands brought out a rudely improvised platform. The girl looked everywhere until she discovered Goade on the outskirts of the crowd. She left her place, walked up to him, and took him by the hand.

"Please come nearer," she begged. "You must hear everything."

He suffered himself to be led to the edge of the platform. Almost immediately afterwards the man and the girl dropped on to their knees. Every one in the congregation covered his eyes. The man prayed. . . . Many times afterwards in life Goade tried to reconstruct that little scene, to feel again the glowing mystery of it, to recollect the almost magical impression of that torrent of passionate words. The old-fashioned market square became an oasis fenced in from the rest of the world. The footsteps of a few passers-by shuffled along the pavements, now and then a motor car with shrill clanging of horn was driven down

the cobbled street, one noisy company of callow
youths went by, shouting and laughing, but all
these sounds seemed to come only as indistinct
echoes from a smaller world. All his old ideas —
the ideas of the cultivated man — of the flamboy-
ant vulgarity of revivalist eloquence, left Goade for
ever, as he stood entranced. The man with the
sobbing voice and the convulsively twitching features was inspired, if ever a man was inspired, and
the girl who stood by his side, her hands clasped
lightly in front of her, her eyes wandering only
from her brother's to his, seemed as though she
were in some way standing upon the altar of sacrifice, as though she were the dumb but passionate
duettist of his pleading. Goade never hesitated to
admit in later years the sweeping down in those
few minutes of all those barriers of cold agnosticism
which the brain builds up against unreasoned
truths. This man had found something, had
found something the world lacked. Goade himself trod the paths of exaltation with that strange
little crowd — the crowd of servant girls, shop
assistants, a labourer or two from the road, a tired
tradesman, a wagoner, a sprinkling of market
women. It was a relief when the voice ceased and
the man fell on his knees. The girl's lips moved
as she prayed, and her eyes never left his. They
were appealing to him spiritually, humanly, wonderfully. Then it was all over. There was a mo-

ment's deep silence. Brother and sister stepped
down, shaking hands with nearly every member of
the congregation. Then they came over to Goade.

"Will you walk with us?" the girl invited.

"Only as far as the door of my inn," he answered. "You must forgive me to-night."

She clung to his arm. The man strode on a
pace or two away, muttering to himself. Somehow
Goade fancied that he was still praying.

"You began to feel," she pleaded. "I saw it in
your face. Oh, don't think that I am ignorant. I
am not. I can imagine the world in which you live.
I know that in a moment even God speaking
through man cannot work a miracle. But you will
come. You will come to us. You will not go away
before we have talked again?"

"I promise," he answered.

"To-night," she went on, "I shall pray for you.
I shall pray with you. If you are sleepless come
to-night. I shall wait for you."

He felt himself shivering with a curious inde-
scribable emotion.

"Very well," he assented, "I shall come."

It was eleven o'clock when Nicholas Goade
started out with Flip in close attendance. In his
hand he carried a thick stick, and he walked all the
time with unusually hesitating footsteps. At the
entrance to the little wood he paused. Through

the trees he could see a single light burning in the caravan. He walked more slowly than ever now, his stick outstretched in front of him, Flip running from side to side. When he reached the last fifty yards, he came once more to a standstill. There was brushwood upon the path which he had not noticed during the afternoon. He took a careful step forward. Suddenly Flip growled, and he realised that the end of his search was at hand. He knocked the loose twigs away with his stick and found what he had expected. He took it up — the innocent-looking branch of an oak tree, unstripped even of its leaves, with cruel jagged-edged knives buried under the bracken on either side of the moss where the foot was meant to fall. He held the diabolical-looking implement gingerly in his hand. Then he walked on to the caravan. As he passed through the gate, he saw the girl waiting and listening, and it seemed to him that she had turned to marble. He threw his burden upon the ground and looked at her without speech. The door of the smaller caravan opened and her brother came silently out.

"For me!" Goade cried, with an undernote of fierceness in his tone.

She held out her hands to him. He would have brushed them away, but he had lost the power. They stole up to his shoulders. She was almost as tall as he, and her face, upturned, was close to his.

"It is the only way," she sobbed out. "Those others, I pleaded with them when they were strong and healthy, and God meant nothing to them. It is only in sickness and suffering that you can reach their hearts. We have found that all our days, James and I. These three young men who have suffered, through their sufferings they have become God's children. You too — to-night it was the beginning, but you would have wandered away, you would have thought all that had happened was just a wave of feeling. You would have gone, as now you will go. I wanted to keep you so much — more than any of the others."

He looked at the wicked-looking device on the ground and still he found speech difficult.

"I am a detective," he said at last. "I was sent here to discover the secret of these accidents."

"And now that you have discovered?" she asked, without loosening her clasped fingers.

He shivered from head to foot — a strong man, a captor of murderers, the man who had faced death as often as any soldier.

"Show me the inside of your caravan," he directed, turning away from her; "the small one."

The man unlocked it, and as he looked around Goade's expression hardened. He stepped back and closed the door.

"You have a stove there," he pointed out. "Bring it to me."

The man obeyed. Goade lit it and placed it underneath the smaller caravan. They collected brushwood sadly. Soon there was a blaze. In the end there was nothing left but charred wood and strange-looking fragments of metal. The smoke was high over the trees. Goade listened.

"In a few minutes," he said, "the people from the village will come. Tell your story as you will."

The girl suddenly clung to him. Her brother looked on with unseeing eyes.

"Don't go!" she sobbed. "You must stay."

There followed an epoch of madness in a well-constructed, logical life!

Half an hour later, Nicholas Goade, with Flip by his side, sat in the Ford car in front of the village inn. The sergeant stood upon the pavement to attend his departure.

"I've decided to travel on by moonlight," the former explained. "Listen, Elworthy. There will be no more accidents."

"You have discovered summat?" the man demanded eagerly.

"Nothing definite," Goade replied evasively. "If anything further of the same sort should happen, I'll make a report in London. My impression, however, is that there will be no more accidents."

"Which way are you going to-night, sir?" the

sergeant enquired, puzzled and disturbed. "It's a queer time to start away."

Goade turned the Ford round so that his back was towards the lights on the hill and the meadow where the caravan was standing. He thrust in his gears and touched the accelerator.

"I'm going as far as I can in this direction before daylight," he answered.

V

WILD MAN'S LOGIC

"FLIP, old lady, you're getting fat," Nicholas Goade murmured reflectively to the small white dog who sat by his side.

Flip, who hated personalities, snapped at a passing fly, and, missing it, yawned. Goade rose to his feet and knocked the ash from his pipe.

"Putting on weight myself," he continued. "We'll leave the car where it is to-day and go for a tramp."

Man and dog presently left the village where they had spent the night and mounted to the moorlands. They left the road and tramped through the sunlit spaces of rich meadowland, skirted a cornfield and followed the wanderings of a trout stream flecked with silver and clear as polished glass. Deserting it when it entered the purlieus of a private domain, they made for the higher land, climbing for an hour or more until they reached at last a plateau of wilder and more broken country, which stretched to the foot of a distant range of hills. Goade, mopping the perspiration from his forehead, threw himself upon the turf with his arms extended and his face upturned to the sun.

"Doing us both good," he murmured lazily.

Flip, who was sitting on her haunches breathing rapidly, suddenly sniffed the heather-scented air, turned her head, and emitted a short bark. Goade turned lazily over on to his side to ascertain the cause of the disturbance. His frame stiffened a little as he watched. He frowned slightly. Presently he scrambled to his feet.

"Looks odd, Flippy," he murmured; "very odd."

A man running in the vicinity of a railway station, pursuing a bus, or with the sombre enthusiasm of an athlete in training, is an ordinary sight enough, but a man running across a great expanse of empty country without any apparent destination, and following no definite track, is a very different matter. Half hidden by the shadow of a rock, Goade watched the approaching figure curiously. The fugitive — if he was a fugitive — was a small, dark man, sombrely dressed and of weedy build. He ran with much effort and in slipshod fashion, his head down, breathing heavily, taking uneven strides, and more than once disappearing altogether from sight as he stumbled into a heather bush. His course, if persevered in, would have taken him thirty or forty yards away from where Goade was standing, but seeing the man and the dog he gave a little cry and turned straight towards them. Almost at that moment, from some unseen place, there came the report of a gun and a shower of small shot pattered into the bushes around. Goade, mounting a little knoll, looked angrily in the direction from which they seemed to come, but there was no indication of any other human being within sight. He turned his attention to the young man who now, with a desperate effort, had covered the last few intervening yards and thrown himself upon the ground close at hand.

"Oh, Gawd!" he exclaimed. "Gawd!"

Flip edged a little farther away. She had no high opinion of the newcomer; neither had Goade. A person more utterly out of touch with his surroundings could scarcely be conceived. He was obviously of Semitic origin, city born, probably a Londoner. His soiled collar, the flashy glass pin in his tie, the thin, pointed shoes, his masses of heavily oiled black hair now hanging in untidy strips about his face, seemed all to belong to the crowded thoroughfares of Houndsditch or Whitechapel. They certainly struck a strangely discordant note in this land of brawny, apple-cheeked men, sunshine, and perfumed open places.

"Gawd!" the young man repeated, struggling to control his sobbing breath.

"What's the matter with you?" Goade asked. "And who was that firing?"

" 'Im, I should think — blast 'im!"

Goade filled his pipe deliberately.

"I may be dense," he acknowledged, "but ' 'im' seems to me a little vague. I should like to know who it was out there in the middle of the moor pattering us with shot."

The young man raised himself upon his elbow; his complexion was a pasty shade of green; he had obviously been very badly frightened.

"Guv'nor," he begged, "you don't 'appen to 'ave a pocket flask with you?"

"I don't carry such a thing," Goade replied. "Plenty of good ale and cider in all the little pubs in this part of the world."

"Not enough on 'em," the newcomer groaned. "Pubs! There ain't even a house in sight. Gawd! I could do with a drink!"

Goade drew out a map and studied it for a moment.

"There should be a hamlet within three miles of here," he remarked. "In the meantime can't you tell me what scared you?"

The young man shuddered.

"Mate," he said, "you've 'eard of wild cats and wild boars and such-like."

"My knowledge of natural history carries me thus far," Goade acquiesced.

The other stared at him.

"You wouldn't be kidding," he declared, "if you'd see'd what I've seen, I've seen a *wild man*. What about that?"

"Good for you," Goade replied coolly. "He seems to have frightened you pretty badly. Tell me about it."

The young man pointed across the moorland towards the belt of hills.

"I'm staying at a farm there," he explained. "Doctor thought I might be turning a bit consumptive. I live in the Bethnal Green Road — name of Bill Aarons. Good for business, but it ain't a 'ealth resort. I come down here for an 'oliday."

"An excellent idea," said Goade. "Go on."

"I got a motor bike and a side car. I didn't mean to bring the side car along, but I thought there might be a bit of skirt 'anging around, so I hitched it on at the last moment. There's a girl at the farm — stand-offish but all right — I tell you, Guv'nor, she's a peach!"

"A girl at the farm," Goade repeated. "Good! We're progressing."

"Can't say as she's seemed partial to me exactly, but to-day, when I was starting for a ride, she said she'd come along. I've arsked 'er often enough before, but she didn't seem somehow to cotton to me. Well, she would go 'er own way — made me strike across a road that wasn't fit for a farm wagon, let alone my outfit. I kept on wanting to stop and talk a bit, but she made me go on until the road ended. Then she got out and stared down this way. 'I'm going to walk for a short time,' she said. 'You can stay here and smoke cigarettes. I may be gone an hour or two.'"

"Not very pally, that," Goade remarked.

"I thought she was kidding," the young man confided. "It's the loneliest part of the moor I've seen — huge boulders of rocks, very little grass even — but she started off. I don't know whether she expected me to follow or not. Anyway, I'd brought her out for the afternoon and I wasn't going to be shaken like that, so I hopped along and tried to take her arm. I thought it would be all right if we rested in the shade of one of the boulders, but she wouldn't listen to me. Mabel Crocombe, 'er name is, and she's a looker, I can tell you. Anyway, we walks along a quarter of a mile or so — I trying to kid 'er on to being a bit pally, and she acting like as though she wanted to shake me. 'You can't go walking about 'ere by yourself,' I told 'er. 'Anything might 'appen to you.' 'You leave me alone,' she snapped. 'I know what I want to do.' . . . Gawd!"

He had recovered his breath by this time, and his body had ceased to tremble. He wiped the sweat from his forehead with a blue silk pocket handkerchief which had seen better days.

"Bill Aarons ain't taking that sort of stuff from any skirt what comes out with 'im, so I just let 'er know it. I had me arm round 'er waist, and I was just pointing out a nice place to sit and talk things over, when, I give you my word, Guv'nor, something came up out of the earth — something that must have been a man, but strike me 'e didn't look it!"

"Out of the earth?" Goade murmured reflectively.

"That's wot it seemed like," the young man maintained. "He just popped out of the middle of that great slanting boulder you can see yonder; must be a kind of cave. Well, 'e made a funny sort of noise and blowed if 'e didn't lift me up by the collar and shake me as though I were a puppy dog. He'd got great brown paws, hair all over 'is 'ead, and, Gawd, I thought at first 'e was naked."

"And was he?"

"He'd no shoes on, or stockings, only a pair of corduroy breeches and a kind of shirt. His skin was pretty nearly black, and when he picked me up he was roaring like a bull. Then he set me down and laid 'old of the girl by the wrist. Mabel shrieked, but she couldn't get away. Then he bellowed to me. 'If you're within sight in ten seconds,' he shouted, 'I'll smash every bone in your body!' Strike me lucky, he meant it, too!"

"What did you do?" Goade enquired.

"What did I do?" the young man repeated scornfully. "That's a good 'un! I legged it, as 'ard as I could."

"And left the girl there?"

"What good could I 'ave done? I tell you, he's a wild man, a giant. His arms were bigger than my legs. He could put me in a sandwich and eat me."

Goade rose to his feet and gazed at the boulder to which the young man had pointed. Even as he stood up there was again the report of a gun from the same direction. Bill Aarons, with a yell of terror, fell flat on his face. This time, however, there was no sound of pattering shot.

"Come on, Flip," Goade called out.

"You ain't going there, Guv'nor?" the fugitive demanded in an awe-stricken tone.

"Of course I am," was the curt reply. "What do you suppose is happening to the girl?"

"Don't you butt in, mate," the young man begged. "You're a big fellow, but 'e could do you in in ten seconds."

Goade, ignoring his companion, started off briskly. The latter hesitated, then followed a few yards behind. Presently he stopped.

"I tell you you're barmy, Guv'nor," he called out.

Goade turned around and looked at him, and the young man slunk behind a rock. . . .

Nevertheless, as he drew near the heap of boulders from which the shot had come, Goade glanced around him a little anxiously. The place was the loneliest he had met with in all his wanderings — a stretch of picturesque but barren country, with nothing to tempt the farmer, either herbage for cattle or soil for planting. There was no road marked upon the map for several miles; a few whortleberry bushes here and there — otherwise neither vegetation nor flowers. One could well believe that months might elapse without even a passer-by. It was certainly, Goade decided, as he neared his destination, a most unpleasant place for an adventure such as the young man Aarons had indicated. He turned the corner of the huge boulder warily, and then stopped short. There was an opening which led underground, which might well have been the entrance to a cave, and in front of it a girl lay stretched upon the ground. . . .

Goade's mind, working swiftly, received several absolutely instantaneous impressions. In the first place, there were no signs of any struggle. The girl's hair — beautiful hair it was, of a light shade of brown — was neat and unruffled. Only her hat — a sort of tam-o'-shanter — had fallen on one side. Neither her country skirt nor jumper were in any way disarranged, but her face was ghastly pale as she lay there moaning. Goade, every sense alert, listened intently as he gazed stealthily around. There was no sound from that opening at the base of the boulder, from which the wild man of Bill Aaron's imagination had without a doubt issued. The girl was alone with the sky above, lying on a carpet of scanty herbage. He leaned over her, felt her pulse, and chafed her hands.

Already she showed symptoms of awakening consciousness.   She was a handsome girl of the best
Devonshire type, largely made but shapely, with
creamy complexion and good features.   Her
mouth, a little open, displayed excellent teeth; her
hands, though brown, were well-shaped and capable.   Suddenly she opened her eyes, and he saw
that they were blue.

"Where am I?" she asked.

"You're quite all right," he assured her.   "On
the moor.   You came with a little man, Aarons.
Had a scare, hadn't you?"

She sat up.   Very slowly she turned her head
towards the narrow opening underneath the boulder, and as she did so he saw the returning colour
fade again from her cheeks.   He assisted her to
her feet and supported her with his arm.

"Lean on me, and try to walk a few yards," he
begged.

"I can walk," she faltered, "but don't leave me."

They moved slowly towards the grassy wall on
the other side of which was the motorcycle.   On
their way they passed a small tarn.   He paused
for a moment, soaked his handkerchief in it, and
bathed her temples.   She drew a little sigh of relief.   Her footsteps became less hesitating.   She
even smiled feebly at Flip, who, with many upward
glances, was trotting importantly by her master's
side.

"Where do you come from, you and your little dog?" she asked.

"On a tramp from Chidford," he answered. "Your escort found us on the edge of the moor. Something seems to have terrified you both. When you feel better, I should like you to tell me about it."

She clutched at his arm.

"It was nothing," she declared feverishly; "nothing at all."

He stopped short. They were close to the gate now, and, making a wide detour round the moor, stumbling on for a while and then hiding, he could see a small, black object — the young man, Aarons.

"But there was something," he persisted. "The young man was terrified. 'A wild man,' he said, who came out of the ground and stopped you both."

"It was just his story," she replied. "I was angry with him because he tried to be familiar. I told him to go, and he went, and then suddenly I felt faint."

Goade was silent for a moment. The girl was a bad liar, but what concerned him most at the moment was curiosity as to her motive. They had reached the bank now on the other side of which was the motor cycle, with its side car.

"I fancy your escort is making his way back," he said. "Shall we rest here?"

She assented. They sat on the bank with their faces to the moor. About quarter of a mile away, Aarons was shuffling down the grass-grown lane towards them.

"So you just fainted," Goade remarked.

"I do sometimes," she confided. "I was sorry that I had come out with that young man. I always disliked him."

"You are sure that nothing else happened to frighten you?"

"Nothing at all."

He looked back at the boulder thoughtfully.

"It's a lonely spot," he observed, "one might easily find a hiding place there."

She shivered.

"Why should any one in these parts want to hide?" she demanded in a low tone. "There isn't a village for miles."

"Some one is hiding there at the present moment," he said quietly.

"How do you know?" she asked with a sort of breathlessness which almost choked her words.

"Well, for one thing," he told her, "the heather just in front had been pushed on one side and broken down by some one passing in and out. There was the imprint of a man's footstep close to the opening, a burnt match, and ——"

"Stop!" she interrupted. "There is no one there. I am sure there is no one there. It was

Mr. Aarons who lit a match and whose footmark you saw."

He looked along the track towards the rapidly approaching figure.

"We'll ask the young man to tell us all about it," he suggested.

She laid her fingers upon his arm.

"Don't," she pleaded. "I beg of you that you don't. Go on your walk, wherever it may lead you. I have a reason for asking."

"I couldn't do that," he assured. "I am too curious by disposition. Your companion has told me that he saw a wild man jump out of the ground. I find you on the spot in a dead faint. It is a situation which must be cleared up."

She withdrew her arm from his.

"You are a very foolish person," she said. "There are many who have lost their lives through curiosity."

He looked back towards the boulder. He almost fancied that the heather bush which partly concealed the opening was moving, as though some one were looking through. The girl was watching him feverishly.

"Perhaps," he reflected, "it would be better if I were to make my way to the nearest police station and bring some one with me."

"Don't do that either," she implored. "Please don't do that."

"There is some one there then?" he asked swiftly.

"I don't know," she answered.   "If there is, why not leave him alone?   What business is it of yours or any one's?   I hate people who interfere."

Mr. Bill Aarons from the Bethnal Green Road came shambling up.

"Strike me, Mister, but you're lucky!" he exclaimed, casting one more fearsome glance across the moor.   "Get in, Miss, if you're ready.   We'll tootle off.   This part of the world ain't 'ealthy."

He bent over the machine, started the engine, swung himself into the saddle and opened the door of the side car for her.

"Now then," he begged.   "Let's get out of this while we can."

The young woman caught hold of Goade's arm.

"I realise now," she said, "you came to help me. You thought that I was in danger.   That was very brave of you.   There was nothing there really to be afraid of, though."

Aarons swung round in his saddle.

"Gawd!" he cried.   "Nothing to be afraid of! You may call me a coward, both of you.   I dessay I am.   I tell you, if ever I see a sight like that again, it'll be the end of me.   Step in, Miss.   If I think of 'im, I'll get the shakes again."

As she took her place she leaned towards Goade.

"Don't go back there!" she pleaded.

"I can't promise," he answered.

She looked at him in obvious distress.

"My name is Crocombe," she said — "Mabel Crocombe. We live at the Wood Farm behind the trees yonder. Will you come and see me?"

He nodded, and stood with his hat in his hand, watching them climb the crazy path, the engine knocking and a little cloud of blue smoke coming out of the exhaust. They completed the ascent, however, and reached the brow of the hill, the girl turning round to wave her hand as they disappeared. Goade filled his pipe and reflected. There was without doubt adventure — it might possibly be an ugly adventure — waiting for him a hundred yards distant. The state of terror to which the young man Aarons had been reduced could scarcely have been attained by normal means. The man who had found temporary shelter in the bowels of the earth underneath that boulder must have some reason for his isolation, some manifest and evil quality to account for the state of collapse to which he had reduced the two intruders. It was a matter which seemed to demand investigation. On the other hand, this was his vacation. There was no particular reason why he should not obey the girl's eager pleading and turn his back upon the whole scene. Logically that seemed to be his only sane course. He arrived at this conclusion, and definitely hammered it into his mind as a basis for action. Afterwards, with a little

sigh, he did what he had known all the time he
would do, he swung over the grassy wall, shortened
his stick in his hand, and, with Flip at his heels,
picked his way across the moor towards the boulder. He paused outside and listened. There was
no sound to be heard. Then he raised his voice.

"Hullo there!"

There was no reply for a moment. He kicked
against the side of the rock. Suddenly a voice
issued from the darkness — a voice which came to
him as a shock.

"Hullo yourself! What do you want?"

"A word with you."

There was the sound now of light footsteps.
Goade drew back, puzzled. The voice which had
answered him had been the voice of no yokel, no
wild, half-civilised creature. It had both the cadence and the quality of a voice belonging to a man
of education. Nevertheless, he stood prepared for
trouble; still half expecting it. Then the heather
bushes were parted and Goade, accustomed to sur-
prises, gasped. A slim, clean-shaven, well-built
young man, in ancient but excellently cut tweeds,
calmly presented himself. He was unarmed and
his single monocle looked as though it had never
left his eye. With one hand he rearranged his
hair which had been slightly disturbed pushing his
way through.

"Hullo, Goade!" he exclaimed. "What the

devil are you doing in this part of the world?"

Goade for a moment was speechless. He looked the young man up and down. There was no doubt that he was a person of cultivation and breeding. With a few slight changes of country to town attire he would have been perfectly in his place in Bond Street or sauntering along Piccadilly. Furthermore his face was not wholly unfamiliar.

"You seem to know my name," Goade said. "I can't say I recognise you."

"We've come across one another once or twice," the other replied. "My name's Erriscombe — Cecil Erriscombe. I was in 'The Brown Mask' at the Royalty. Some one brought you round the first night."

"I remember, of course," Goade admitted. "All the same, you must forgive me if I seemed a little taken aback. The last person I expected to see crawling out of a hole in the earth was a popular *jeune premier*. What the devil are you doing here, man?"

Mr. Cecil Erriscombe smiled. He produced a gold case, selected a cigarette himself, and extended the case to Goade.

"To tell you the truth," he confided, "I'm sick of all ordinary holidays. I was doing a tramp across the moors and I came upon this place in a thunderstorm. I thought it would be a jolly good idea to settle down here for a week or ten days, and try nature at first hand. You remember I was in 'The Arcadians,' and the idea always rather appealed to me. I bought some stores and moved in a week ago. I've had a thundering good time, but I'm off to-morrow."

"God bless my soul!" Goade muttered, still a little dazed.

"My bathtub has been the tarn there," the other continued, leaning back on the boulder where they were seated, and watching the smoke from his cigarette curl upwards; "also my looking glass. I've a few odds and ends inside, but nothing worth speaking about. The only thing I regret is that I haven't had a camera to take me in my make-up."

"In your what?"

"In my make-up," the young man repeated coolly. "You see, the first day I was here, a tramp tourist and then some children picking whortleberries annoyed me and spoilt my idea of what complete solitude should be, so I wired to London for an aboriginal disguise *à la* George Robey — tomahawk and all — and I've had some fun," he concluded, with a grin, the genuineness of which his companion for some reason felt inclined to doubt.

"I should say you have," Goade remarked, his sense of puzzlement increasing. "You've frightened a young man out of his senses, and I found a girl in a faint outside."

"I'm sorry about that," Erriscombe declared.

"I meant to frighten the young man, but when I heard nothing more of the girl I thought she'd made off in the other direction. She didn't cry out or anything, or I should have heard it. She's all right now, I hope?"

"She's all right," Goade assented tonelessly. "She's gone off home with the young man."

"And, by Jove," Erriscombe reflected, with a queer little smile, "won't the countryside be prowling round here in a day or two to see the wild man. I think I'll leave the outfit to amuse them, and clear off. What part are you making for, Goade? We might as well push on together."

"I thought of calling first at that farm behind the trees there," Goade replied, "just to let the young lady know she's nothing to be terrified about. Afterwards I've got to get back to Chidford where I left my car."

"Chidford will do me all right," Erriscombe agreed with obvious eagerness. "What about your going up to the farm, as you want to, and picking me up on your way back? I've got a few oddments I might put in my knapsack. Anyway, it won't take you more than an hour there and back. We shall get to Chidford in time for a glorious high tea.   I'm not sure that I shall be sorry to sleep inside sheets again."

"All right," Goade acquiesced.   "I'll be glad to have you — take you along in the car to-morrow,

if you like. Let's have a look at your quarters,"
he added, peering through the heather bush.

The young man indulged in a slight grimace.

"I'd rather you didn't," he confessed. "I'm by
way of being a little fastidious, and it's more than
ordinarily stuffy and untidy down there. I've
slept out of doors the last two nights."

Goade nodded thoughtfully. Suddenly Flip
darted past him through the opening and disappeared in the gloom. A moment later he heard
her sharp bark from down below.

"What is it, Flip?" he called out.

There was no reply. Instead, Flip's bark suddenly changed into a howl. Erriscombe's fingers
which held his cigarette shook.

"For God's sake, call the little beast," he begged.
"What a hideous sound."

Goade rose to his feet and looked at the young
man by his side gravely.

"I've only once before heard her howl like that,"
he said. "I'll have to go down, Erriscombe."

The young man stood motionless.

"What do you mean?" he asked, after a moment's pause.

"I'll have to go down and see what my dog's
howling at," Goade explained. "Sorry, Erriscombe."

He suddenly gripped him by the arms and felt
him all over.

"All right," he added, as he released him. "You can wait for me, if you like, or come."

Erriscombe shrugged his shoulders and produced an electric torch from his pocket which he handed to Goade.

"You'll want that," he said. "Be careful of the third step. You needn't be afraid. I'll wait for you."

Goade took the torch and stumbled down. The air was good enough, and at the bottom of the three roughly cut steps the floor was carpeted with dried heather. There was a place in the corner where some one had apparently slept, a few dirty cooking utensils, and a basin which had been used to bring water from the tarn. Goade's first glance around showed him these things; his second, something far more horrible. From a recess, leading apparently into an extension of the cave, stretched a man's leg, roughly booted, hairy, and tanned by the sun. Goade crept forward and flashed on his light. A large, scantily dressed man, with a huge crop of hair and beard, lay motionless upon his side. There was a faint smell of gunpowder in the air, a gun and empty cartridge case upon the floor, a little wisp of blue smoke still lingering in a distant corner. Goade stood upright for a moment, looking around him. Then he turned slowly away and mounted the steps into the daylight. Erriscombe was seated upon the boulder, the sun flashing upon his monocle, but as Goade appeared he rose to his feet as though to greet some one. Goade, coming gasping into the sunlight, rubbed his eyes for a moment. A few yards away, the girl was hastening towards them, her arms outstretched.

"Cecil!" she cried. "Cecil!"

The young man shook his head slowly. She came sobbing into his arms.

"It couldn't be helped, dear," he said. "Goade happened along, and that's the end of it."

"You'd better neither of you say anything more," Goade advised them. "You know who I am, Erriscombe. I'm on a vacation, but I'm still an officer of Scotland Yard all the same. I'll have to take you back to Chidford."

Erriscombe nodded. The girl was seated upon an adjacent boulder, rocking slowly in her misery.

"That's all right, Goade," the young man said. "I shall give you no trouble. As to keeping silent, that's my affair. I have a fancy to tell you exactly what took place, here on this spot, with Mabel listening."

"It's against my advice," Goade reminded him.

"Last summer," Erriscombe went on imperturbably, "I came down here for a holiday. I stayed at Wood Farm. How shall I put it in plain words? I became attached to Mabel, who was, I believe, half engaged to that clod down there — son of a farmer at Chidford. Do you remember anything, Goade?   A newspaper case?   We kept it fairly quiet, but the Sunday papers got hold of it."

Goade nodded.

"I begin to remember," he acknowledged.

"Well, I wasn't quite the blackguard some people thought me because I came from London and was an actor.   I went away for a time, and Mabel left to stay with an aunt in Exeter.   We were married, and I came back here to complete my holiday.   We made a mistake, of course," he went on, "in not announcing our marriage, but I was due to open at the Haymarket a month later with a part which was to have been the part of my life.   I knew that it would mean permanent success for me, and I knew that I would have a better chance if I kept my marriage secret until after the show was thoroughly started.   Of course people gossiped a little about us, but Mabel didn't care; she knew it would be all right directly.   The trouble came with that brute with whom I have just squared matters."

Erriscombe paused and looked up to where a hawk was circling overhead as though wondering what was going on below.   Then he continued.

"This man — Crang, his name was — went about the country like a crazy loon, and every one warned me to be careful.   He tracked us one day and found us out here.   I did my best, but what was the good of it, Goade?   He is six feet six, with the muscles of an ox, and, although I could box a bit, it's never been one of my hobbies. He pounded me pretty well into a jelly — thrashed me, Goade, with Mabel running screaming about. Have you ever been thrashed?"

"I don't know that I have," Goade admitted.

"Well, I tell you it's hell. I had about half an hour of it before the blackness came. Then he must have given me a few kicks before he left me. There was no first night at the Haymarket for me. I was in Exeter Infirmary for a month, and Crang went to prison for two years —'Attempted Manslaughter.' "

There was another silence. A solitary curlew had drifted across the sky with mournful little calls. Mabel had begun to sob, and Goade waited gravely. He intended now to hear every word.

"You've never been thrashed, you said, Goade?" Erriscombe recommenced. "There's something in a man's blood seems to turn sour at the thought — something in oneself, I suppose, born at one's public school, and carried through the 'varsity into life. I have always known what the consequences would be. I knew there was only one thing to bring me peace of mind again, and I've done it. I had to kill the man who thrashed me. A fortnight ago I read that he'd broken out of prison and was supposed to be hiding somewhere around. I felt I knew where I should find him. I travelled down

here.   I had a revolver, but I didn't use it.   You'll
find it in the tarn there.   I shot him with his own
double-barrelled gun."

"Who fired the first shot at Aarons?" Goade
asked.

"Crang," Erriscombe explained.   "It was Mabel and her little cockney who drew him out of his
lair.   I was lying waiting a few yards away —
waiting for him to come out.   Mabel hurried from
the farm to stop the mischief if she could.   Crang
heard their voices and came up.   He scared the
little man out of his life, had a shot at him, and left
the gun against the boulder.   Whilst he was talking to Mabel I got it.   He heard me and turned
around.   I shot him.   It was all I could do to
drag him down to his hole, but I did it.   Just as I
was coming up again I heard you, so I waited.   I
invented the story about the George Robey outfit
because I knew Aarons would tell you what sort of
a man it was who had frightened him.   Now, what
are you going to do about it?"

"I don't know," Goade confessed.

They sat and looked at one another.   Erriscombe rose to his feet and crossed to his wife's side.
His arm went around her waist, and her head sank
upon his shoulder.

"I had to do it, dear," he whispered.   "It's a
load gone — a great load."

"Let's make sure that the man's dead," Goade

suggested, after a brief pause.   "Come and help me Erriscombe."

They descended the steps and dragged the heavy body into the outer cave.   Farther they were incapable of moving him.   Goade stripped off his coat, examined the wound, and turned abruptly around.

"Fetch some water in that basin," he directed. "He's not dead."

For half an hour or more Goade worked, cutting up his own shirt to make a bandage.   Erriscombe had some brandy, a few drops of which they forced between Crang's teeth at the first sign of returning consciousness.   Finally Goade staggered out into the fresh air.

"The man's as strong as an ox," he announced. "He may live.   In fact, I feel sure he will."

"And now?" Erriscombe asked again.

"And now?" the girl repeated, her eyes fixed upon Goade.

"Can you drive a car?" the latter enquired.

"Any make," was the confident reply.

Goade pointed across the moor.

"You'll find my car there," he indicated.   "Take it and drive round to the farm.   Send a wagon and all the strong men you can find down to the lane there.   That young man Aarons can mount his motor cycle and fetch a doctor.   You'll have to leave the rest to me.   I'll do the best I can."

He held out his hand which Erriscombe gripped. No words passed between them; only a single glance of understanding. The girl went bravely off by her husband's side. Goade waited until they were out of sight. Then he made his way to the tarn and fetched more water. When he returned and descended the three steps, the man's eyes were wide open. Goade sprinkled his forehead, felt his pulse, and sat down by his side.

"You've been shot," he said.

"Aye," the man muttered.

"If I were you," Goade went on, "I should forget it."

The man looked at him vacantly.

"You slipped coming down the steps, carrying your gun. It went off and you were hit. I came along and found you. You see, you're a Devonshire lad; you understand fair play. You half killed Erriscombe. He can't fight, but he had to get it back on you. You're quits now. He's married to Mabel. Nothing can alter that."

The man lay quite still. His features twitched. He looked as though he were trying to understand.

"You haven't seen Erriscombe to-day," Goade persisted. "You've been alone all the time until I found you. I heard the gun go off, and I came across. You'll get well, but they may ask you questions. You're a sportsman, Crang, I'm sure. Keep your mouth shut, and I'll do my best to help

you for breaking jail. I'm a head man at Scotland
Yard, and I've influence there. You understand?"

"If the chap's married right and proper to Mabel," the man said slowly, "I don't wish 'e no more
harm. I fell down them steps, master. That's
right. I aren't seen Erriscombe. I got it now.
Gi'e me some more water."

Goade held the bowl to his lips. Then he
listened.

"They're coming to fetch you," he announced.
"You'll be all right, Crang. You'll stick to it?"

"I sure-ly will," was the emphatic reply. "It
were ordained they should marry, and you can tell
Mabel it's all right."

The man's strength was amazing. He was almost able to sit up. Goade made his way out to
the fresh air, and beckoned to the labourers who
were already climbing out of the wagon in the lane.

VI

"QUEER thing, coming across you outside the Cathedral like that," Captain Faulkener remarked, as he established his two guests — Flip was of the party — at a comfortable table in the coffee room of the Cathedral Arms. "Only last night I was thinking about you."

"We really wandered down this way quite by chance," Goade observed. "I hadn't meant to come so far south."

Faulkener ordered his luncheon and sipped his apéritif.

"Jolly good idea of yours," he remarked, "to spend this six months' leave wandering about quietly. The most tranquil county I know, Devonshire."

"Is it?" Goade murmured. "I was thinking of trying Mexico."

"Eh?"

"I mean to say that somehow or other Flip and I always seem to be nosing our way into other people's troubles. We've had one or two quite strenuous weeks in the most unlikely places."

"You certainly did see through that Unwin affair," Faulkener admitted. "Shocking thing, too! Where are you going from here?"

"We haven't any plans," Goade admitted. "Now I'm so far south I daresay I shall make for the coast."

A man, passing down the room, paused to exchange a word with Faulkener, who introduced him presently to Goade.

"This is Mr. Goade from Scotland Yard, Manton — Major Manton, the governor of our prison here."

"I know Mr. Goade quite well by name and reputation," Major Manton declared.

They talked for a moment indifferently. Then the latter passed on, and Captain Faulkener leaned towards his companion confidentially.

"I didn't ask him to lunch, Goade," he said, "because I wanted just a word with you privately."

"Not another case, I hope," Goade asked.

"No, not exactly that," Faulkener replied, after a moment's hesitation. "There's a little matter here, though, that's bothering me. I'm hard up against it, and the person chiefly concerned doesn't want me to appeal to Scotland Yard. I thought perhaps, as you were in the neighbourhood — if I could interest you — you might see if you could straighten it out for us."

"Tell me about it," Goade invited resignedly.

"I'd rather you heard the story — from the person chiefly concerned. You can spare half an hour this afternoon?"

"I suppose so," Goade assented without enthusiasm. "I meant to spend the rest of the day here, anyhow."

"I'll put your name down at the club," Faulkener suggested. "There's a decent rubber of bridge there in the afternoon. Can you be ready for me at four o'clock?"

"Certainly. You won't tell me anything about the case, then?"

"Not a word."

At four o'clock Faulkener led the way to the Close, and rang the bell of a very picturesque old red brick residence, ivy-covered and with a strong ecclesiastical flavour. A dignified butler answered their summons and ushered them into a spacious library, where a tall and rather pompous-looking man, with the nether garments of a dignitary of the Church, was seated at a handsome writing table dictating letters to a secretary. He waved her away and rose to welcome his visitors.

"Dean," Captain Faulkener said, "this is Mr. Goade, of whom I have spoken to you. Mr. Goade — Dean Followay."

The Dean shook hands, and indicated two comfortable easy-chairs.

"I haven't said a word to Goade yet about this little trouble," Faulkener went on. "I thought I'd like him to have the details from you in your own words. If I might venture to advise you, Dean, I'd keep nothing back from Mr. Goade. You'll find," he continued, turning to his companion, "that the case is just as simple as it is embarrassing."

The Dean inclined his head. He had a long, rugged face with an unusually large mouth, shaggy eyebrows and iron-grey hair. Without being exactly of ascetic appearance, he certainly gave one the impression of a man whose lines had not always been cast in the easy places.

"I think," he began, his finger tips pressed together, his eyes fixed upon Goade, "that my friend Faulkener has used the right term to describe our position. It is embarrassing. I shall tell you the story of our predicament in as few words as possible, but it is necessary to enlarge for a moment on matters of my personal history."

"I should like you to tell it to me in your own way," Goade said.

"I started life as a curate with no private means," the Dean continued; "I have never been possessed of private means. I have a large family, and my stipend has at no time left room for luxuries. The care of my children, therefore, becomes an important matter to me. I have four daughters, the

eldest of whom is twenty years old.   I will be quite
frank with you, Mr. Goade.   It is our ambition —
the ambition of their mother and myself — to have
them comfortably settled in life.   There is not a
great deal of young society in this neighbourhood.
For this reason, my wife and I were exceedingly
gratified when a fortnight ago we received an invitation from the Duchess of Exeter for our daughter to join her house party at Exeter Park for
three or four days.   Our daughter made her prep-
arations and duly departed.   She received the
most delightful hospitality, but she returned here
on the termination of her visit in a state of great
distress."

The Dean paused for a moment, and played
thoughtfully with his watch chain.

"I should explain," he went on, "that my daughter Florence had a godmother, a great friend of my
wife's — the Princess Shibolzky, an English lady
married to a Russian.   We always hoped, as the
Shibolzkys were very wealthy and had no children,
that my daughter might benefit by the association.
The revolution, unfortunately, changed all that.
The Princess died in something approaching poverty.   She, however, left to my daughter Florence
the one remaining piece of her famous collection of
jewels — an emerald pendant of great beauty and,
I believe, great value.   We only received the jewel
a month ago.   A local jeweller valued it at some

two thousand pounds, and when the invitation from
Exeter Park arrived I was making enquiries with
a view to having it insured.   Against my wishes
my daughter decided to take the jewel with her.
She had, it appears, a green evening dress, and the
effect of the jewel, I must admit, was exceedingly
pleasing.   I confess that I should have had it insured before allowing her to depart with it, but I
did not.   She came back without the jewel, and
with a very distressing story.   It is a story of a
few words only, and it is one which she shall tell
you herself."

The Dean rang the bell.

"Will you ask Miss Florence to step this way,"
he instructed the butler.

The young lady duly appeared — a dark, handsome girl, almost as tall as her father, but without
in any other way resembling him.   The Dean introduced her, and Captain Faulkener placed a
chair.

"I want you to tell this gentleman, Mr. Goade,"
her father said, "how you lost your jewel.   You
must tell him exactly what you have told us."

She made a little grimace.

"It is a horrible business," she said, "but this is
just what happened.   The platinum clasp was
very strong indeed, and could be opened only by
pushing the two ends together.   Several people
admired it, and Lord Geoffrey, who danced with

me quite a lot, seemed particularly struck with it. Towards the end of the evening he asked me to sit out on the terrace with him. There was a slight breeze, and he insisted upon fetching me a wrap. We talked for some time, and more than once I saw the jewel flashing, and even remember now thinking what a wonderful colour it seemed against my dress. When we went in, Lord Geoffrey unfastened my scarf himself. He was quite a long time doing it, talking to me all the time, saying, in fact, rather nice things. He left me inside the room and took the scarf away. Before he came back some one had claimed me for a dance, and I had scarcely started it before I noticed that my emerald had gone — chain and all."

There was a short silence.

"I won't waste your time, Miss Followay, asking useless questions," Goade observed. "You believe that Lord Geoffrey took it?"

"What else can I believe?" she asked. "It was he who insisted upon the scarf, which was really unnecessary. He was a long time drawing it away, talking in a rather bewildering manner all the time. He went off directly we entered the ballroom — and the emerald was gone."

"You spoke to him about it, I suppose?"

"I did, as soon as I could find him, but, though I looked for him everywhere, he seemed to become invisible for at least an hour. No one seemed to know where he was. When at last I discovered him, he was in the room where wine and refreshments were being served, sitting alone. I went up to him at once and told him that my emerald was gone. I had already searched the terrace thoroughly where we had been sitting, but he insisted upon going back there again. I suggested that he should look in the scarf, and he went and fetched it, but there was nothing there. He seemed very distressed, and he promised me that he would do everything he could, but he begged me not to make too much fuss at the time, as the Duchess, who is very old-fashioned, detests anything of that sort."

"The Duchess," the Dean explained, "belongs to the old-fashioned school. The idea of a jewel robbery in her house would have filled her with horror. It is quite certain that my daughter would never have been invited there again if we had put the matter in the hands of the police in the usual way."

"She was told, I suppose?" Goade asked.

"Naturally. Florence mentioned it as casually as possible before leaving the next morning. Even then the Duchess seems to have been very cold about it."

"I tried to explain that it was valuable," Florence interposed, "but she simply said that, if it had been dropped when dancing, the servants would find it and it would be returned. If they did not find it, I would probably discover it amongst my belongings when I returned home."

"I know nothing about the family," Goade admitted.   "Are they wealthy?"

"Sufficiently so, I believe," the Dean replied, "but, with the present iniquitous system of taxation, no member of the old peerage or the landed gentry can be described as being wealthy.   However, I imagine that the Exeters are well enough off even for their position."

"And this young man, Lord Geoffrey?"

"From all that one hears, one would consider him a remarkably well-conducted young man for his position in life," the Dean replied.   "He is the eldest son, and represents the Southern District of the County in Parliament.   He is spoken of as a very promising young politician."

"Any private means?"

"So far as I know, none, except his allowance from his father, which is, however, no doubt adequate."

Goade reflected for a moment.   Suddenly he looked across at the young lady.

"And now tell me the rest of the story," he suggested pleasantly.

She started, visibly perturbed.   A little flush of colour came into her cheeks.

"What do you mean — the rest of the story?" she demanded.

"You are keeping something back," Goade complained. "Nearly every one does. It is such waste of time if they really require help."

She remained silent for several moments.

"Well, there is only this," she admitted at last: "I met Lord Geoffrey when I was staying in London with my godmother before she died. He became quite attentive to me. It was through him, I am sure, that I was asked to Exeter Park. Since that night, however, he has not called or been near me. He was not there to say good-bye when I left in the morning. He seems deliberately to have avoided me. I couldn't help telling him about my loss, especially as he was with me when it happened. He seemed, however, to resent it."

"A little unreasonable on his part," Goade commented.

"Decidedly unsportsmanlike," Faulkener murmured.

"The point is, however," the Dean confided, "that the young man is expected here this afternoon for tea. He was lunching with the Bishop to-day, where my wife was also a guest, and she invited him. He accepted after some hesitation, I understand."

"I should rather like an opportunity of seeing him," Goade acknowledged.

"That opportunity will be forthcoming," the Dean said.

"And in the meantime, Miss Followay," Goade enquired, "which would you prefer — the return of your jewel or the exposure of the thief?"

She hesitated.

"I should like my jewel back, of course," she admitted. "I should like also to make the thief confess."

The butler threw open the door.

"Tea is served in the drawing-room, sir," he announced.

"You will join us, I trust, Mr. Goade?" the Dean invited. "You will then have an opportunity of meeting this young man."

They crossed the hall and entered a very pleasant drawing-room; with French windows leading out on to the lawn of the Close. Goade was presented to Mrs. Followay, a handsome but tired-looking replica of her daughter, to a clergyman and his wife, and to Lord Geoffrey Fernell. The latter was a young man, tall and thin, with a slightly studious air and a reserved manner. He conversed very little with any one. Even when Florence went over and sat by his side he seemed to unbend very slightly. He discussed a recent session in the House of Convocation with the visiting clergyman, and exchanged a few words with the Dean upon a Bill which he had supported dealing with some ecclesiastical matter. His manner, however, was marked all the time with a certain

aloofness.   He was the first to leave, and after he
had gone Mrs. Followay sighed.

"I can't think what's happened to Lord Geoffrey," she declared in a melancholy tone.   "It almost seems as though you had offended him, Florence."

Florence set down her cup and turned towards
the door.   It appeared to Goade, who opened it
for her, that there were tears in her eyes.   He
heard her run up the stairs, and she waved him
a little adieu with one hand, her handkerchief in
the other. . . .

"A nice girl," Faulkener remarked, as the two
men strolled across the Close towards the club.

"Very nice indeed," Goade assented.   "I like
her better than the young man."

"I think she's got hold of a mare's nest, all the
same.   The idea of a man in Lord Geoffrey's position robbing a girl for the sake of a trifle like that
isn't credible.   What do you think, honestly,
Goade?"

"I agree with you."

"That's what makes the whole thing so difficult.
The Followays want to recover the emerald, naturally.   On the other hand, they've already irri-
tated the young man, and they're deadly afraid
of upsetting the rest of the family.   You see, they
absolutely dominate Society down here, and old
Followay's got three other daughters coming on.

That's why he was so anxious to have a word with you. He daren't come to us officially. He doesn't want to offend the Exeters, but he does want his emerald. There you are, Goade. It's up to you."

"Thanks," Goade remarked drily. "Looks so easy, doesn't it?"

Goade spent a lazy few days in the meadows and around the quiet countryside adjoining the city. He bought a fishing rod and took lessons with some success from a piscatorial expert. He also painted assiduously for several afternoons. On the fourth morning he received a budget of communications by the midday post. He went through them, whistling softly to himself. Presently he rang up Faulkener, who appeared without undue delay. They strolled into the coffee room for lunch.

"Well, my friend," the Chief Constable enquired, "how is the great work proceeding?"

"Somewhat unexpectedly, to tell you the truth," Goade confessed. "I know all about Lord Geoffrey Fernell. Apparently — and I have every confidence in my dossier — there are few better conducted young men in this world. His chambers — in the unfashionable Adelphi, by the way — are looked after by old retainers of the family — a man and a woman of unblemished respectability. His life is one which would pass the censor in every respect. He is assiduous in his attendance at the

House, and a valued member of various committees. He is also on the Boards of two hospitals, one charitable institution, and one perfectly sound commercial undertaking. The young man, as you see, therefore has interests. He attends the theatre, but he eschews musical comedy. He is a strenuous golfer, an occasional polo-player, although this season I understand that he has taken to tennis instead. His friends are all of a highly superior class. He has no entanglements, and, so far as one can gather, no extravagances. The Duke of Exeter should be congratulated. He has apparently — so far as this dossier goes — a perfect son. There will be a perfect hereditary legislator to follow in his footsteps."

"That sounds all right," Faulkener observed. "Anything else?"

Goade proceeded with his lunch for a moment in silence.

"Unfortunately," he admitted, "there does appear to be another trifling incident on the other side of the ledger. Without the slightest doubt on the seventh of July — that, I think, was the day after the dance at Exeter Park and the day upon which Lord Geoffrey returned to London — the emerald pendant lost by Miss Followay was pawned in Holborn for one thousand pounds by a young man giving the name of Geoffrey Fernell and answering in every respect to the appearance of Lord Geoffrey."

"God bless my soul!" Faulkener gasped.

"It just shows us," Goade continued, stooping down to pat Flip, "the hypocrisy that exists in our very midst. There are points about this matter which probably are puzzling you as they certainly are puzzling me, but I imagine that by proceeding calmly everything will be made clear to us in the end."

Faulkener looked up at his companion suspiciously.

"I say, Goade, you're not kidding or anything, are you?"

"I was never more serious in my life," was the prompt assurance. "I've done what you asked up to the present. I have made all my enquiries unofficially, and I have discovered what you wanted to have discovered. The Dean has now the whole position before him. As a Christian and an upright man, I presume that there is only one course open to him."

"You mean that he'll have to prosecute?"

"What else can he do?" Goade argued. "The young man appears to have behaved damnably. He was attracted by Miss Followay in London. When meeting her at the house of the Princess Shibolzky, he imagined her to be a young woman of wealth. Down in the country he discovers her to be the daughter of an impoverished Dean, existing under the patronage of his family. He helps

himself to her one possession, convinced — and
rightly convinced, as it seems — that the Dean
would never dare to put the matter into the hands
of the police for fear of offending the great family
of the district.   I didn't like that young man,
Faulkener, the moment I saw him."

"But your dossier?   What could he want a
thousand pounds for?   Apparently he doesn't
race, drink, gamble, or keep women."

Goade nodded thoughtfully.

"Men have strange ways of getting rid of money
sometimes," he observed, "and even a Scotland
Yard dossier has its limitations.   In the meantime
what about it all?   Are you coming round with me
to the Deanery?"

"I suppose I had better," Faulkener observed,
a little dubiously.   "You must remember, however, Goade, that your visit must still be entirely
unofficial."

"We'll all go unofficially," Goade agreed —
"even Flip."

At a somewhat early hour that afternoon a for-
midable assemblage of visitors was ushered by the
butler into the stately library of Exeter Park.
Florence entered first, pale but determined.   She
was followed by the Dean, angry yet nervous.
Faulkener, considerably embarrassed, came next,
and Goade, with Flip — who had evaded the servi-

tors at the door — under his arm, brought up the
rear. The butler waved them to chairs. If he
felt any surprise at this unusual visitation his face
showed no signs of it.

"His Grace shall be informed of your presence,
sir," he announced, with a little bow to the Dean —
after which he took his leisurely departure.

The four maintained a grim silence during their
period of waiting. Presently the door was thrown
open, and an elderly lady, so true to type that she
reminded one of Du Maurier's Duchesses of *Punch*
repute, entered the room, followed by a long, lean
man with frosty blue eyes, a thin mouth, and a gla-
cial bearing. The visitors rose to their feet. The
Duke and Duchess shook hands with the Dean and
his daughter in perfunctory fashion, accorded
some sort of salutation to Captain Faulkener, and,
after a glance of cold surprise, ignored Goade.
The Duchess seated herself in a comfortable chair;
the Duke stood by her side.

"To what," the latter asked, scrutinising the
little group through his eyeglass, "are we indebted
for this, may I say, unexpected visitation?"

The Dean took the floor, and at the sound of
his own voice he felt better. It was a voice which
had awed the sixth form of a great public school,
which had rung through the halls of many a Church
Congress, which had earned for him his stole, and
would probably earn for him a bishopric.

"Your Grace," he said, "I can assure you that it is with the greatest reluctance I have come here this afternoon. Nothing but a strong sense of duty could have induced me to have intruded upon you and her Grace or to have brought to your notice a matter as disagreeable to ourselves as I am sure it will be painful to you."

The Duchess raised her lorgnettes for a moment and closed them with a snap.

"Has your daughter come to make a fuss about her bit of glass?" she asked coldly. "My servants have already had orders to restore it as soon as it has been found."

"That bit of glass, as your Grace calls it," the Dean continued, "is a very valuable emerald pendant bequeathed to my daughter by her godmother, the Princess Shibolzky. There is, I fear, no chance of your servants being able to restore it, for its presence has been discovered in a pawnshop in London. I may add that, notwithstanding your Grace's disparaging reference to it, the jewel was pawned for a thousand pounds."

"And by whom?" the Duke asked.

"I regret to say, your Grace, by your son," the Dean announced, pausing for a moment to give his words full effect.

It was, at any rate, an achievement to have surprised two people who seemed incapable of feeling of any sort. The Duchess's expression was one of disdainful horror. The Duke's jaw had fallen a little, and incredulity was written in every line of his face.

"By my son! By Lord Geoffrey!" the latter gasped at last. "I never heard anything more ridiculous in my life. Dean, are you aware of what you have said? Am I to look upon you as being concerned in this — I can only call it conspiracy?"

"Your Grace," the Dean replied, "the facts are as I have stated them. My daughter was appalled at her loss. She feared to speak plainly in your house, but on her return to the Deanery she admitted frankly that the pendant was lost during the few moments when Lord Geoffrey withdrew a scarf which, without any ostensible reason, he had insisted upon her wearing. I sympathise with my daughter's sensations. She was confident that the jewel was in your son's possession, but she felt herself utterly unable to deal with the situation beyond announcing her loss."

"Let me understand this matter," the Duchess said. "There will be more to be heard of it later. Steps will be taken. I understand you to say, Dean, that your daughter, on returning from her unfortunate visit here, confided to you that her pendant was lost, and expressed the opinion that it had been stolen by Lord Geoffrey?"

"That is true," the Dean admitted. "I cross-

questioned my daughter in every way, but there
was no shaking her conviction."

"Let her speak for herself," the Duchess continued, with all solemnity. "Young woman, have
you come here to accuse my son of having stolen
your pendant? My son! Lord Geoffrey! The
heir to the Dukedom!"

"I didn't want to come," the girl replied, with a
little tremor in her voice. "If Lord Geoffrey had
asked me for the pendant I should have given it to
him. The fact is, though, that he took it. I felt
practically certain that his fingers undid the clasp
when he was taking that wrap away. Almost
directly after he left me I saw that it was gone.
Now it has been discovered in a pawnshop in Holborn, pawned under the name of Geoffrey Fernell."

The Duke moved slowly across the room and
rang the bell.

"There is only one way to end this unpleasant
scene," he announced. "You shall repeat your
statement to Lord Geoffrey himself."

There was a brief silence. The butler entered,
and was requested to invite the presence of Lord
Geoffrey. During the interval the Duchess once
more raised her lorgnettes to her eyes.

"And who is the person with that disgusting
little white dog?" she asked.

"Your Grace," Goade replied, "I regret that
my presence is an offence to you, or the presence of

my dog. I can assure you that I am here against my will. My visits are often paid in that way. My name is Goade — Inspector Goade of Scotland Yard."

The Duchess' hand trembled. She turned towards the Dean, and her voice should have terrified him almost more than it did.

"You mean to say," she demanded, "that you have had the wickedness, the colossal impertinence, to place this matter in the hands of the police?"

"Your Grace," the Dean confided. "On the evidence before us, I might reasonably have considered it my duty to have done so. As a matter of fact, however, Mr. Goade is here unofficially. We consulted him as a friend of Captain Faulkener's. Our only desire was that the matter might be cleared up without undue delay and without publicity."

The Duchess was speechless. Just at that moment the door opened and Lord Geoffrey entered. He was in tennis clothes, and carried a racket under his arm. For a moment, as he stared through his monocle in surprise at these unexpected visitors, he bore some slight resemblance to his father.

"Hullo!" he exclaimed. "Why, how are you, Miss Followay? How are you, Dean? I wanted you for tennis, Faulkener. What's this happy little gathering all about?"

"You may well ask, Geoffrey," his mother said sombrely. "You will remember that it was at your solicitation that we invited Miss Followay to spend a few days with us recently."

"Well, what about it?" the young man enquired.

"You may also remember," his mother continued, "that Miss Followay mentioned something about having lost some article of jewellery — a pendant, I think it was?"

"I remember it quite well. We had the place thoroughly searched, but the thing couldn't be found."

"The Dean is here this afternoon to inform us that the article in question has been discovered in a pawnbroker's shop in Holborn," the Duchess declared — "discovered, it appears, through the agency of the gentleman with the dog, who comes from Scotland Yard. These people assert that the jewel was pawned by a young man giving the name of Geoffrey Fernell."

Lord Geoffrey stood for a moment as though turned to stone. Then he threw his racket on to a settee.

"My God!" he exclaimed.

"At present," the Duke interposed frostily, "your mother and I have not made up our minds whether to consider this as an outrage or a simple act of lunacy on the part of these good people.

We should like to know what you have to say."

Lord Geoffrey said nothing at all. He stood for several moments with his hands in his pockets. Then he turned suddenly towards Florence.

"Did you think I took it?" he demanded.

She faced him bravely.

"I did," she replied. "I didn't want the scarf. You insisted upon bringing it to me, and when you took it off I felt your fingers on the clasp of the pendant. You took the scarf away, and I believe the pendant was in it. Anyway, you went to London the next morning, and the pendant was discovered pawned for a thousand pounds in your name."

He ignored the others and looked only at her. She met his gaze without flinching.

"If you suspected me, why didn't you mention it before?" he asked.

For a moment she hesitated; not, however, with any sign of embarrassment.

"It was my first visit here," she explained. "I didn't wish to cause trouble. I hoped that my jewel might have been returned."

"I think," the Duchess suggested coldly, "that we had better bring this most unpleasant meeting to an end. Is there any further question you would like to ask my son?"

Goade, who had been patting Flip absently for several moments, suddenly intervened.

"I should like, if I may, to ask him a somewhat obvious question," he said. "I should like to ask him whether he stole Miss Followay's pendant?"

"I thought you had already discovered that," was the unexpected reply. "Yes, I stole it."

"And pawned it in Holborn?"

"Quite right."

There was a tense and most amazing silence. Even the Dean gasped. The Duchess was simply incapable of speech; the Duke, a most undignified looking figure, stood with his mouth open, gaping across at his son.

"Might one further enquire why you stole it?" Goade continued.

"I needed the money," was the curt admission.

The young man faced his father and mother, both of them now almost in a state of collapse.

"Of course, I'm terribly sorry and all that," he said, "but after all, I wasn't the only one to blame. I have written you time after time, Dad, and told you that it was perfectly impossible for me to keep up my position upon an allowance of two thousand a year. I needed a thousand pounds very badly, and I thought I saw a way of getting it without running any risk. I meant to have returned the thing to Miss Followay later on."

The Duchess seemed to have lost all power of consecutive reasoning. She had become a limp, unbalanced person.

"You stole!" she murmured. "Geoffrey! Our son! You stole from a girl!"

"The trinket," the Duke announced tremulously, "shall be returned."

"I am not quite sure," Florence said coldly, "whether that will meet the case. You do not know, Duchess, or you, Duke, exactly why Lord Geoffrey asked that I should be invited here. I should like to tell you. I saw quite a great deal of him in London. Since he came down here I don't think that he has treated me very well. One hears now that he has become attached to a young lady in London at the Duke of York's Theatre. Did you steal my pendant to buy presents for her, Lord Geoffrey?"

The young man turned towards the door.

"I've had enough of this," he declared sulkily.

He would have left the room, but Goade intervened.

"I am afraid, Lord Geoffrey, that I cannot permit you to leave just yet," he announced.

"What do you mean?" the Duchess gasped.

"Your Grace," Goade said gravely, "your son has confessed to a theft. If Miss Followay desires to prosecute ——"

"Prosecute!" the Duchess shrieked.

"Prosecute!" the Duke groaned.

"Why not?" Florence rejoined. "Your son has treated me very badly. He paid me a great deal

of attention in London, and has simply ignored
me here.   It seems to me to be the natural course
to take."

Lord Geoffrey led her a little on one side.

"With your permission," he said, turning to his
father and mother, "I will discuss this matter with
Miss Followay.   I will give my word to this gentleman," he added, turning to Goade, "not to leave
the place."

He threw open the door, and they left the room
together.   The Duchess turned to the Dean.

"Dean," she begged, "I think that you had better perhaps add your persuasions to the persuasions of my son.   I rely upon you to see that your
daughter does not remain obdurate.   If Geoffrey
took the trinket at all he must have taken it as a
joke."

"He could scarcely have pawned it as a joke,"
the Dean pointed out stiffly.

There was an awkward silence.   Then the door
was opened.   Florence and Lord Geoffrey entered.
The latter wore an expression of great relief.

"It's quite all right," he declared, addressing
his father and mother.   "Florence admits that it
was a joke.   She is perfectly willing to say no more
about it.   We are sending the announcement of
our engagement to the *Morning Post* to-night."

The Duchess looked across at Florence with an
icy gleam in her eyes.

"So this is your price!" she exclaimed.

The Dean rose to his feet with dignity.

"Your Grace," he said, "if you take that attitude ——"

The Duke intervened.

"My wife forgot herself," he apologised. "Anything is better than what might have happened. My dear," he went on, taking Florence's hand, "let me wish you happiness. Geoffrey, I congratulate you."

Geoffrey patted his father on the back and whispered in his ear. The Duke nodded.

"I will see my lawyer to-morrow," he promised. "You shall have a town house and an adequate allowance."

Captain Faulkener rose to his feet; Goade followed his example. The Duke looked at the latter anxiously.

"Under these circumstances, sir," he said, "I presume that no further action on your part will be necessary."

"I am in Miss Followay's hands," Goade replied.

"And I," she murmured, "have made terms with the enemy." . . .

Lord Geoffrey clambered into the car going home and seated himself between Goade and his fiancée.

"Goade," he confided, "you were damned good."

"I was what?" Goade enquired.

"Damned good," Lord Geoffrey repeated.

"You played the Scotland Yard sleuth marvellously. Difficult people mine, but you scared them all right."

Goade pinched Flip's ear for a moment.

"You two young people," he remarked, "did quite well. There were times when I scarcely realised myself that the whole thing was a plant."

VII

THE HONOURABLE MURDERER

GOADE, driving the little Ford car with his luggage strapped on behind and Flip seated by his side, reached the outskirts of the city of Exeter on his way southwards. Flip, after a vigorous exchange of ferocious amenities with a dog of similar species attached to a fishmonger's barrow, had settled down to watch with appreciation the slowly unfolding landscape, with its promise of haystacks, rabbit burrows, and other delights. A young man, doubled up on a motor cycle, suddenly shot out from the dwindling traffic, passed them with a rapid series of explosions, and drew up about fifty yards ahead. He descended, leant the cycle against a tree, and, stepping into the road, held out his hand. Goade brought his car to a standstill, and the young man approached, touching his hat awkwardly.

"Can I have a word with you, sir?" he begged.

Goade looked at him curiously. He was very pale, very thin, indifferently, almost shabbily dressed. His features were insignificant, as was his whole appearance.

"Haven't I seen you before somewhere?" Goade enquired.

"You may have seen me in the yard or about the Cathedral Arms, sir," the young man replied. "I am the chef there."

"Well, what do you want with me?"

"Just a word if you'd allow me, sir. Could you bring your car to the side of the road. It will take a matter of a minute or two to say what I want to."

They were just past the tram terminus and at the foot of a gentle ascent of smooth road, bordered on each side by the gardens of prosperous-looking villas. Goade did as he was asked, and stopped his engine.

"Now what is it?" he enquired.

"It's about Ed Thorne, sir," the young man confided. "You remember about him."

"I can't say that I do for the moment," Goade acknowledged.

"He's the young man as is to be hung next Thursday week unless the Home Secretary reprieves him. He killed a man one night in the yard of the Cathedral Arms — hit him over the head with a mallet."

"I remember," Goade assented. "What about him?"

"Well, he didn't ought to be hung, sir," the chef said earnestly. "There's been summat kept back in that case, sir. They made Ed out to be just a drunken brute who was jealous because Hawkins had got his job.   There was more in it, sir — more in it than ever came out."

"I don't remember the case," Goade confessed. "That generally means, where I am concerned, that it was a one-sided affair.   I suppose this man Thorne had a lawyer."

"He had a lawyer all right, sir, but he wasn't no good to Ed because there was no one as could get Ed to open his mouth."

"What's your name?"

"Alfred Mace, sir."

"Well, why do you come to me, Mace?" Goade enquired.   "His lawyer's the only man who can do anything.   It's too late for any outside inter-ference."

"It's like this, sir," Mace explained eagerly. "There's no one can say anything against the firm of Bulliver & Bulliver.   They're the best lawyers we've got in Exeter, but Mr. Ernest Bulliver who took this case on, he's more of a parson than a lawyer — if you follow me.   He's as stiff and un-bending as though he were fed on parchment.   He wasn't the sort of man Ed was likely to cotton to. He just asked Ed if he'd anything to say, and Ed said 'No.'   He didn't go round trying to find out for himself if there wasn't something else that might be brought forward.   He just took Ed's word, and that meant practically no defence at all.

His counsel made a speech full of long words and argued out law cases to make the jury believe it was a case of manslaughter, and he left it at that."

"Do you know something about this that no one else does?" Goade enquired.

"I rightly don't, sir," was the prompt admission, "but I know this much: there's summat that no one knows except Ed which would make things look different."

Goade had intended lunching at Totnes. The young man's earnestness, however, was compelling. He leaned back in his seat with a sigh of resignation, drew out his pipe, and commenced to fill it.

"Tell me about the case," he invited.

"It doesn't sound much, sir," Mace confessed. "Anyway, listening to what there was at the trial won't take you long.   Ed Thorne had been boots at the Cathedral Arms for eight years, and he was kind of keeping company with the young woman who was chambermaid there — Kitty Fields her name was.   Ed was a lively sort of chap, always good company, and fond of gadding around.   He used to take a drop occasionally, but nothing to harm him.   Then there was this other chap, Hawkins.   He drove the bus at the Cathedral Arms. Well, everything was all right until he began to court Kitty Fields.   Suddenly Ed took to drink and got the sack, and Hawkins got his job.   He began to take Kitty Fields out regular, but all of

a sudden she changed her mind — wouldn't have
anything to do with either of them, and said she was
going out to an aunt in Canada.   She left sudden-
like, and four days afterwards Ed — who had
found another place but wasn't living any too
steady — came into the yard of the Cathedral
Arms, swinging that b——y hammer.   He went
straight up to Hawkins, said something which nobody heard, and fetched him one on the head that
would have killed a ox.   That's all there was to it."

"Well, it looks simple enough," Goade observed.
"I'm sorry for your friend, Mace, but, you see,
bringing that hammer in with him, and walking
straight up to the man who had got his job and
killing him — well that's murder, isn't it?"

"It's murder all right, sir," Mace acknowledged.
"I ain't denying that; no more ain't any of Ed's
friends.   But there's what you call extenuating
circumstances.   That's what you get a reprieve
for, isn't it?"

"That's so," Goade assented, "but in this case
where are they?"

The chef leaned forward, his dirty-white hands
gripping the side of the door.

"Mr. Goade, sir," he said, "it's my belief as there
were something more in it.   Ed was quiet enough
after he'd lost his job.   He didn't say naught
against Hawkins, and Kitty Fields, she'd gone off;
but, if there's one thing I'll swear to God upon, it

is that Ed had some other reason for killing Hawkins, and it's that other reason as might provide
the extenuating circumstances."

"What makes you think so?"

"For one thing," Mace went on eagerly, "I was
leaning out of my scullery window to get a little
fresh air, and I seed Ed come along. Hawkins
didn't take any particular notice. He and Ed
were on pretty good terms. They'd had a drink
or two together the night before, but as Ed came
near he said something — I couldn't hear the
words, but I saw Hawkins start. I saw him look
scared to death, Mister, and then Ed hit him.
Gawd, he did hit him too!" the young man concluded with a little shiver.

"And that's all?"

"That's all. But, Mister, I tell you, Ed never
ought to swing. Some one ought to make him say
what else it was he'd got against Hawkins."

"I'm afraid it's a pretty hopeless affair," Goade
decided slowly.

"Don't say that, sir," the chef begged. "Just
go and have a word with Mr. Bulliver. If it was
only imprisonment I wouldn't say nothing, but I'd
a pal once who was a warder at the jail. I've seen
them gallows. Ugh!"

The young man dabbed at the perspiration upon
his forehead. He was out of condition, and he
shivered a little, notwithstanding the heat. Goade

looked down the long, sunny road and sighed.

"Well, I'll tell you what I'll do," he conceded. "Major Manton's a friend of mine. I'll go back and have a word with him. From what you've told me of the case, however, I tell you frankly that I don't think there's a chance."

"Mister," the other said earnestly, "maybe there ain't. I only know that I'll feel better afterwards for having had a try, and I think you will too. If there's anything you want to see me about, you'll find me in the Cathedral Arms, sir. I'm not reely off duty to-day, but when I heard you'd gone, I had to start out after you."

Goade nodded, turned round, and drove back to Exeter. He made his way direct to the prison, rang the imposing-looking bell, and was duly conducted into Major Manton's apartments. The latter welcomed him with some surprise.

"Hullo, Goade!" he said. "I thought you were off this morning."

"Well, I did start," Goade replied, "but I got held up. Tell me — you have a man here, Thorne, under sentence of death."

Manton nodded.

"Poor chap, yes, and I'm afraid he'll hang, too."

Goade recounted his adventure of the morning. Manton listened attentively, but his expression was a little dubious.

"Of course, if there was anything else between

the two men," he commented when Goade had finished — "anything that really reflected discredit upon Hawkins, Thorne might have a chance, simply because of his war record, which was damned good. It was the only thing they had to urge in his favour, however, and it was a pretty thin petition."

"When do you expect the reply from Whitehall?"

"Well, they have to keep it a day or two. Let's see, to-day is Tuesday. I should think they'd probably keep it there till Saturday. We shall get it back on Monday, and, unless anything fresh turns up, I'm afraid it's five to one against a reprieve."

"I suppose you could get me a few minutes with this man Thorne?"

"Of course I could, if you like."

"I'd better do the thing properly," Goade reflected, "and see his solicitor first."

"Bulliver & Bulliver. You'll find them next door but one to the hotel. Pretty starchy card, Ernest Bulliver. If you decide to step over and have a word with Thorne, be here at three o'clock, and I'll see to it." . . .

Goade made his way to the solicitor's office. He waited for a quarter of an hour in a dingy waiting room whose walls were hung with the announcements of sales and plans of building lots. Eventually a lanky youth took him out into the passage, opened one of several doors, and ushered him into a very solemn and bare-looking apartment. A tall, thin man rose from behind a desk to greet him — a pale man, with black hair, rather long, but plastered down at the sides and at the back. He was dressed in sombre clothes, and resembled a super-verger.

"Mr. Goade," he said gloomily, glancing at the card. "Kindly be seated."

Goade accepted the chair which was offered and laid his hat upon the table.

"I am not professionally interested in the case, Mr. Bulliver," he began, "although, as you will gather from my card, I am connected with Scotland Yard. I wanted to have a word with you, however, about this man Thorne."

"Perfectly hopeless affair," Mr. Bulliver declared, leaning a little back in his chair. "I couldn't get the shadow of a defence out of him. All that he said to me from beginning to end was: 'I meant to kill the man, and I'm glad I did.' "

"He never specifically stated the reason, I suppose?"

"Never," the lawyer replied. "One concludes that it was because Hawkins had supplanted him in his post. That class of person, I daresay, regards those matters very seriously, and there is no doubt that, without having had sufficient to drink to confuse the issue, Thorne had been drinking before he worked himself up to that murderous frame of mind."

"There was a girl," Goade ventured, "to whom both men were attached."

"Quite true. I caused enquiries to be made. She, however, had left for Canada before this regrettable event, and it transpired in the course of my enquiries that the two men had been together and on moderately friendly terms many times since she had left the hotel."

"That makes the affair seem more hopeless than ever," Goade admitted. "With whom did the girl live whilst in England?"

"With her uncle and aunt — Morton by name. If you wish for their address, I can provide you with it. In fact, I happen to remember it: One Ash Farm, Trawlee. Trawlee is about sixteen miles from here — rather an out-of-the-way place."

"Thank you very much," Goade said, rising to his feet. "I presume if I should think it worth while to have a word with the prisoner, you would have no objection?"

"Not the slightest," Mr. Bulliver assured him. "A petition for a reprieve has gone up as a matter of course. I fear the result is hopeless. Good morning, Mr. Goade."

At a few minutes after three that afternoon

Goade, accompanied by the governor, was ushered into the condemned cell — one of three cut off from the remainder of the prison and a little larger than those in general use.   Thorne, a well-set-up young man with good features, but with terrible lines about his face, was seated at a table by the side of a warder.   There was a box of dominoes before him, but it was unopened.

"Thorne," Major Manton announced, "this is Mr. Goade of Scotland Yard.   A friend of yours has interested him in your case, and he would like to ask you a question or two."

Thorne's mouth tightened.

"It is very kind of the gentleman," he acknowledged civilly, "but there's no use in asking me questions.   I have nothing further to say."

Goade seated himself on a bench opposite.   For a moment he studied the condemned man in silence.

"Have you any relatives, Thorne?" he asked.

"No very near ones, sir."

"Near or distant, you ought to think of them in a case like this," Goade pointed out.   "There's a petition for a reprieve, as I daresay you know.   As things are at present, I tell you frankly that I do not think the reprieve will be granted."

"I never thought it would, sir."

"What is necessary," Goade continued, "to give those who are anxious for your life to be spared a chance, is that there should be extenuating circumstances discovered for your attack upon Hawkins.   Were there any?"

"None that I can mention, sir," was the firm reply.   "The dog deserved to die, and he's dead."

"Why did he deserve to die?" Goade demanded.

"That's my business, sir."

"Your refusal to answer that question," Goade said, "will cost you this last chance of your life. You realise that?"

"Perfectly."

"It is no use changing your mind," Goade warned him deliberately, "at the last moment — the night before you are to die, for instance.   It would be too late then.   You realise what 'too late' means?"

"I do," Thorne assented, almost defiantly.   "I faced death most days for years out in France for the sake of killing a German or two I didn't particularly hate.   I'll face death a good deal more cheerfully for having sent a man out of the world who didn't have no rightful place there."

Goade rose reluctantly to his feet.

"You won't tell me what those last words were that you said to Hawkins before you killed him?"

For the first time Thorne showed some sign of emotion.

"There wasn't any one heard them?" he asked quickly.

"No one heard them," Goade admitted, "but the little chef at the Cathedral Arms — Alfred Mace — was leaning out of the scullery window, and he heard you say something."

Thorne was obviously relieved. He even smiled.

"Good little Alf!" he murmured. "He's the right sort, Alf! I bet it was he started you on this."

"It was," Goade admitted. "What was it you said to Hawkins? Come on, Thorne. Don't be obstinate. Give yourself a chance. Life's worth having for a young fellow like you."

Thorne shook his head.

"You mean kindly, sir," he said, "but you're wasting breath."

The Governor put back his watch. He laid his hand on Goade's shoulder.

"Time's up, I'm afraid," he announced.

"And a good job too," Thorne declared. "I don't mean that unkindly, sir," he added, turning to Goade, "but I've finished with everything, and it don't do me no good to be made to think. I'd as soon to-morrow was Thursday week as not."

They left him then; Goade, especially, with regret. There was nothing else to be done.

"Hopeless sort of chap," the Governor remarked. "I wish to God we could do something to help him. I hate my job on Thursday week like poison."

"I wish I could save you from it," Goade reflected. "I like the fellow."

At five o'clock that afternoon Goade drove up to the front door of one of the barest and gloomiest-looking farmhouses he had come across in the county. It was plainly whitewashed in front, without a scrap of garden or vegetation of any sort. There were weeds growing almost out of the wall; a general air of poverty everywhere. Goade's summons was answered after a moment's delay by a tall, round-shouldered man, white-bearded and white-whiskered, with lowering forehead and forbidding expression.

"Mr. Morton?" Goade enquired.

"That be my name," the man replied. "I don't know you."

"My name is Goade. Can I come in for a moment? I want a word with you."

"What about?" the farmer demanded. "If you've come about them machines ———"

"I haven't," Goade interrupted. "I want to speak to you about your niece, Kitty Fields."

The man stood back from the door and led the way into the kitchen. A woman was seated in a high-backed chair, knitting. The floor was of bare stone, the table and dresser of common deal. There was not even a hearthrug in front of the fire. The whole place carried out the promise of the exterior — cold and poverty-stricken. The farmer jerked his thumb at Goade.

"He's cum abaht Kitty," he announced.

"What about her?" the woman asked.   "She's in Canadie."

"Will you give me her address, please," Goade begged.

"Why?" the farmer demanded.

"I am not at liberty to say for the moment," was the guarded reply.   "It is certainly for nothing to her disadvantage."

The phrase sounded suddenly legal.   There was a gleam in the old man's eyes.   The woman laid down her knitting.

"Might it be a legacy?" the former enquired.

"It's sure-ly old Margaret over to Parracombe," the woman put in.   "She were worth a tidy bit."

Goade remained silent.   The woman rose and took an envelope from underneath a teapot upon the chimney piece.

"There it be," she said.

"It's a powerful long way off," the farmer pointed out.   "Ten days for a letter there, and ten for a reply.   Is it naught we can have any concern in?"

Goade carefully pocketed the envelope, and evaded a direct response.

"Have you heard from your niece since she reached Canada?" he asked.

The woman shook her head.

"Kitty was no scholard," she said.   "She'll write some day."

"What boat did she go on?" Goade persisted.

"It wur the boat as left Southampton July 1st," the old man declared. "*Arrytoba*, or summat like that."

"And when did your niece leave here?"

"Two days afore. She'd summat against Exeter, and she wouldn't go there, so she had to drop down to Foulsham and take a train from there. She took the carrier's cart to Foulsham on the Thursday as the steamer sailed on the Saturday."

"Was your niece engaged?" Goade enquired.

"Not as I knows on," the woman answered, a little doggedly. "She was never one to talk about her affairs."

"She never spoke, for instance, of a young man named Hawkins, or another called Ed Thorne?"

"Never spoke of any young man at all," the farmer declared. "Might it be a matter of a legacy?" he persisted, with a sudden gleam of cunning in his eyes.

"I may have to come and see you again," Goade replied. "If so, I'll tell you more about it then."

He took his leave, somehow glad to be in the fresh air again. Flip, who had been on a voyage of investigation, came flying round the corner, pursued by a flock of geese. Inside the room, the farmer and his wife sat looking at one another in chilly silence.

Four glorious days of summer passed, days during which Flip ought to have been smelling for rats under haystacks, or attempting to insinuate her fat little body into the utterly inadequate refuges of the elusive rabbit. Goade himself should have been endeavouring to reproduce on canvas the shadows on the Dartmoor moors, the sedater beauties of sheltered homesteads, or the purple glories of the encircling hills. The Fates, however, had ordained things differently. Flip and her master remained in Exeter: the former frankly and unaffectedly bored; the latter, as he pieced together the fragments of a commonplace story, a little wearied, yet all the time in some measure inspired by that curious background — the saving of a man's life. On the evening of the fourth day he felt justified in sending a special despatch to his Chief at Scotland Yard:

"Please see Home Secretary re *petition for reprieve of Edward Thorne, lying under sentence of death at Exeter Jail. Let matter remain in statu quo until you hear from me to-morrow or next day. Fresh influence of motive possible which may affect decision."*

On the fifth day Goade knocked at the inhospitable door of One Ash Farm. The farmer came to him from the stack yard, looking mouldier than ever in a suit of threadbare corduroys.

"You be here again?" he observed, in a tone of questioning hostility. "Be there any news of that legacy?"

Goade looked at him coldly — a strange, depressing figure he seemed, with that covetous gleam of the eyes, the hard, thin lips. The front door opened and the farmer's wife also presented herself. She was holding a potato in one hand and a paring knife in the other.

"Is it about the legacy?" she demanded, peering at him through her steel-rimmed spectacles.

"I have brought you news of your niece," Goade replied.

"From Canadie?" the old man asked.

Goade shook his head.

"Your niece," he confided, "never went to Canada."

"Eh?"

"She left here, as you told me, to take the carrier's cart to Foulsham. She told the carrier she would wait for the bus. She told the bus she was going by the carrier. She never sailed upon the *Arizona*. She never went to Canada. She never went more than a quarter of a mile away."

The farmer and his wife drew close together.

"Who be you what know all that?" the former demanded.

"I'm a detective officer from Scotland Yard," Goade said, "and, on behalf of the poor man who lies sentenced to death in Exeter Jail, I have made it my business to discover your niece's whereabouts. The night she left your house she went no farther than the pit which you call the 'Bottomless Tarn' on the other side of the lane.   She drowned herself there.   They are bringing the body here now."

He pointed to the little company who were carrying a gate, upon which lay something covered by a piece of sackcloth, up that flinty, barren drive. The sun flashed upon the buttons of their uniforms. The farmer shivered.

"What passed between you three the night she left," Goade continued, "no one, I suppose, will ever know.   You may have understood, or you may not; but, if you refused to receive her living, you can scarcely refuse to receive her dead."

The farmer groped his way towards the front door and held it wide open.   The melancholy procession crossed the threshold.   Goade started up his car and Faulkener climbed in with him, taking Flip on to his knee.

"I've left the Inspector in charge," he said. "There's nothing to be done there.   You've got the letter?"

"I've got it in my tin fly-case," Goade replied. "The ink's run, of course, and it's a sodden mess; still, I hope we'll be able to make something of it. The address is clear enough, anyway."

"For Hawkins?" Faulkener asked.

"For Hawkins," Goade assented.

Faulkener, who rather prided himself upon his limousine, held on to the side of the car.   He had slipped a little upon the smooth upholstery, and was being badly jolted.

"I say, Goade," he complained, "why the devil don't you get a decent little car?"

Goade laughed softly.   Flip, who was exceedingly uncomfortable, had leaned over to lick his hand on the steering wheel.

"I expect for the same reason," he replied, "that I am not keen about a really thoroughbred dog."

Late on the following afternoon there was a little commotion in the cell where Thorne still sat, like a man slowly drifting into a state of mummification.   An outside warder had sent in a message.   The attendant rose to his feet.   He cast a pitying glance at his companion.

"The governor," he announced.

Thorne rose a little wearily to his feet.   Already in imagination he had so often been through the hideous anticlimax, which, out of sheer kindliness, his warders had explained to him.   The governor came in, but his expression was scarcely what the warders had expected.

"Thorne," he said, "I am happy to tell you that the petition for your reprieve has been accorded a favourable hearing by the Home Secretary.   Your sentence has been commuted to penal servitude."

Thorne stood there with twitching hands and twitching face. Into his eyes there seemed to have crept a wonderful light. He looked past the governor out of the walls into the sunlight. Manton afterwards confessed, when he could be induced to talk of that moment, that he had never felt so small a being.

"Reprieved!" Thorne repeated. "Why?"

The governor took a step forward. He leaned towards the bewildered man; his tone was very kindly.

"Thorne," he continued, "now I come to bad news. The young woman with whom you once kept company — Kitty Fields — has been discovered drowned in a pit near her uncle's farm. Upon her was found a letter addressed to Hawkins, the man you killed."

Some part of his unnatural strength seemed to desert the man. He trembled visibly. The governor made a sign to the warder by his side, and they assisted him towards a chair.

"Sit down, Thorne," the governor enjoined. "The letter was a terrible condemnation of Hawkins. She spoke of having sent word to you, of having told you the truth, of having told you, too, that she was about to become a mother. What did you do with that letter?"

"I swallowed it after I had killed Hawkins,"

Thorne confessed after a moment's hesitation. "I killed him a quarter of an hour after I had read it."

There was a silence. Never since he had entered the condemned cell had the man faltered. Manton saw the collapse coming, and turned away.

"We sha'n't keep you here as long as you fancy, Thorne," he said, raising his voice a little. "You'll have years of freedom later on. You can change his cell at once," he added, turning to the chief warder. "Look after him well." . . .

Goade pulled up the car by the side of the road. They were in a very beautiful country lane twenty miles away from Exeter. On one side of them was a hedge, from which the late honeysuckle still drooped; on the other a field of gold. Flip made a dart for a promising-looking corn sheaf and yelped with delight at the bolting of a rabbit. Goade, strolling after her, threw himself upon the stubble, and produced from his knapsack a flask of whisky, a bottle of Perrier, a tumbler, his pipe, and a tobacco pouch. He mixed his drink with the air of a man who has earned it. Flip's ecstatic yapping was the only sound to be heard except the twittering of some birds in the hedge and the distant humming of a corn-cutting machine.

"Well, thank God we're clear away this time!" Goade murmured, as he raised his tumbler to his lips.

VIII

FROM the depths of the sylvan repose and the almost uncanny quiescence of the winding lane which curled its way around the side of Tanton Beacon and dropped into the valley beyond, Goade, in his little car, still hot and puffing with the long climb, passed suddenly into an atmosphere of drama. The last turn had brought into view a prosperous-looking farmhouse, built of grey stone with low, mullioned windows overgrown with ivy, and red-tiled roof, soft with age. The place had an air of prosperity. There were at least a dozen fat stacks, a large orchard, the trees of which were laden with fruit, a well-kept looking farmyard, a row of labourers' cottages at a decent distance. In the lane just outside the front gate stood a tall man, dressed in farmer's homespun clothes, breeches and gaiters, a man of somewhere about fifty years of age, ruddy of complexion, at times, perhaps, benevolent of appearance, but just now a man possessed by an ungovernable fit of rage. His right hand gripped a riding whip by the butt. There was murder in his blue eyes as he gazed at

the man who was standing a few yards away, close
to a small yellow caravan from which he had apparently descended. The latter's black hair, his
olive complexion, his lounging, self-assured bearing, were all characteristic of the gipsy. He stood
with his back to the broken window of his caravan,
and, though he seemed not to have troubled to put
himself into an attitude of defence, his eyes were
stealthily watching the farmer. Goade, his brakes
smelling hot from the long and winding descent,
drove on a few more yards, and came then perforce
to a standstill as the caravan, one wheel of which
was already in the ditch, blocked the way. As he
sat there for a moment, he realised that the two
men who had first engaged his attention were not
the only persons concerned in the little drama. A
couple of farm labourers, looking sheepishly ill at
ease, were standing a few yards away from the
caravan, and, farther in the background, leaning
upon the gate and looking out upon the scene with
apparent amusement, was a tall, largely made
woman, with smoothly brushed black hair and
flashing brown eyes. She wore a rose-coloured
gown — a strange piece of colouring in the landscape of greens and golds. Her lips, parted now
in a lazy smile, were almost unnaturally scarlet.
She had the air of a pleased onlooker, and she appeared to view Goade's arrival with disfavour.
The latter, with a little sigh, descended from his

car. For a brave man — a man who had never
shirked a fight when it was necessary — he disliked disturbances of all sorts. His superficial apprehension of what was passing seemed to him to
presuppose a commonplace and sordid little
tragedy. The farmer had probably married a
gipsy, and this was one of her former companions
come to beg, borrow, blackmail, or perhaps to re-
visit an old sweetheart. Flip, trotting importantly at her master's heels, and sensing something
unusual, glanced from side to side as though to
realise its cause, permitting herself a short bark of
enquiry. Goade translated her curiosity into
words.

"Is there any trouble here?" he asked. "There
is scarcely room for me to pass."

"If those men of mine had the guts of rabbits,"
the farmer declared angrily, "they'd topple his
b——y caravan into the ditch and make room."

The supposed gipsy turned towards Goade with
a whimsical smile.

"You perceive," he remarked, "that for no reason I can imagine I have become an object of dis-
taste to this worthy farmer. I never saw him before. I cannot conceive in what manner I can
have offended him. Yet on my applying at the
house for assistance — you see I have had the mis-
fortune to get one of my wheels in the ditch travers-
ing this abominable lane — I seem to have stumbled

into a veritable hornets' nest. You appear to be a reasonable person, sir. Ask him yourself in what way I have offended. Ask Madame there, who mocks me from the gate, whether she has ever seen me before. Ask those two clumsy-looking louts hanging about behind why they refuse to help restore my — shall I call it caravan? — to a state of equilibrium."

Goade stared at the speaker for a moment without reply. His attire was homely enough, but after all the tweed coat was well-cut, and the remnants of a shabby tie were suggestive of some well-known colours. His shirt, though of coarse flannel, was clean; the knickerbockers and shoes, although ancient, might well have been those of a country gentleman. More significant still, the voice with its slight drawl was most distinctly the voice of a person of culture.

"What's wrong?" Goade asked the farmer. "Why don't you let your men help move the wagon?"

The woman suddenly lifted the latch of the gate and strolled out. She walked with delightful freedom and a faint swaying of the hips suggestive of foreign origin. Goade watched her in unwilling admiration.

"I will tell you," she said. "My husband spends half his days and nights in terror of the gipsies. Why, I do not know, for I am one and they are people without evil in their hearts. And yet I do know. Shall I tell these gentlemen, John?"

"You can tell them what you damn well please," the farmer answered surlily.

"My husband has no manners," she sighed, "and his temper is bad. Now I will tell you why he becomes furious when a gipsy passes the house."

She paused for a moment. She had addressed herself at first to Goade. Now she turned from him and her eyes sought the eyes of the other man.

"A year ago," she recounted, "there came along this way an old woman telling fortunes — a poor old soul she was, but with those things in her which none can understand. It was harvest time and my master there was merry. He would have his fortune told and mine, and he heard what I think has sometimes made his life a torture to him. The woman told him that the day would come when I should leave his roof, and the man who carried me away would be one of my own race."

Again she paused, and her eyes, as she laughed across at the stranger of the caravan, were aflame with a curious light. There was mockery and challenge there, also a shade of wistfulness. She shrugged her shoulders.

"Your fortune teller was indiscreet," the man of the caravan remarked, smiling.

"B——y old witch!" the farmer muttered.

"Alas," she went on, "the mischief was done when

first she opened her mouth. My husband believed her. Since then he has lived in terror of the day when the prophecy should come true. That, sir," she concluded, "is the cause of his inhospitality, though why he should take you for a gipsy, except that you have the dark hair and skin, and the caravan of a pedlar, I cannot say. Are you a gipsy, Mr. Pedlar?" she demanded, with an insolent little toss of the head.

Once more the eyes of the two met across the road, and this time the farmer's grip of his riding crop tightened.

"Madame," the man replied courteously, "if I am a pedlar, see my wares."

He unfastened one side of the yellow travelling van, disclosing the interior. There was not a single article of merchandise visible of any sort — a neatly rolled-up little bunk, one or two water colours and prints upon the walls, bookcases filled to overflowing, a small stove and a cupboard full of crockery. The farmer drew a step nearer and looked in, frowning. The woman boldly leaned head and shoulders through the open space.

"It is a very pleasant home," she murmured. "I take back my words, sir. I do not believe that you are a pedlar."

The air of strain seemed to have departed. The farmer stood sheepishly in the road. The owner of the caravan tapped a cigarette against one of the wheels and lit it.   Goade, who was quick to notice such things, realised that the tobacco was of choice quality.

"The fact of it is," the stranger confided, "that I don't know how to peddle, or perhaps I might. My efforts at making a living — a very necessary thing to me, for I am a poor man — are confined to a little — well, I will dignify it and call it literary work.   It was in my attempt to conclude a short article on this part of the country that I forgot to watch where I was going, and allowed this patient but unenterprising beast of mine to shy at a cockerel and place me in this unfortunate predicament."

"I think the best thing we can all do," Goade suggested to the farmer, "is to help him get clear. His wheel is sinking lower every moment."

"If he'd said at first that he wurn't no gipsy," the farmer grumbled, "there'd have been naught of any disturbance.   No gipsy will I have around the place, or on my land, which is well known, and them as calls my wife a gipsy lies.   She's naught to do with them, or of them.   She's my properly wedded wife, as all should know who live in these parts, and, if she were gipsy-born afore, she be naught now but a proper Devon woman.   Come on Bill there, and you, John!   Put your shoulders to it."

The united efforts of the little company, aided by the horse, succeeded in bringing the caravan into the middle of the road. The farmer glanced towards Goade.

"You'd best turn in at my gate for a minute," he advised. "It's a narrow part here, narrow even for one wagon with a team. You can drive round the front of the house and out'en the gate top end of meadow, and you'll be ahead of him. If you don't do that you won't be able to pass for a matter of three miles."

"The farmer's advice is good," the owner of the caravan agreed. "I am a slow traveller. I find it restful."

The incident appeared to be at an end. The labourers trooped off. The farmer stepped back and opened the gate for Goade.

"What do you think on 'im?" he asked confidentially. "He has the quality speech, but he be as much like a gipsy as any I ever seed."

"It is clear," Goade replied, "that he is a person of education. I think I shouldn't worry any more about him."

Goade drove through the farmyard and round the front of the prosperous-looking house. The woman stood by the other gate. She opened it for him, and as he drew near she laughed up into his face.

"Give me your little white dog," she begged. "I need company here."

Goade shook his head.

"I couldn't part with her," he said, "I should be too lonely."

"Lonely!" she replied, lingering a little over the word. "No man ever knows what loneliness really is."

He passed through the gate, raised his hat, and waved his hand to the owner of the caravan who was seated, ready to start. At the top of the long ascent, Goade found the water in his radiator boiling and stopped for a moment. He looked backwards. Only the woman remained, leaning against the gate in almost the same attitude as when he had seen her first, except that her head was turned in his direction. Somewhere between him and her the caravan was slowly mounting the hill.

An hour or so later, Goade was eating bacon and eggs and drinking beer in the small coffee room of the King's Arms at Dunstowe, when he was attracted by the resounding echo of heavy hoofs passing underneath the arched entrance outside into the inn yard. He glanced up. It was the caravan with its owner upon the box seat. A few minutes later the latter strolled in and greeted Goade pleasantly.

"Like the tortoise," he announced, ringing the bell, "I have arrived."

"Are you spending the night here?" Goade enquired.

The newcomer ordered a double glass of sherry and some supper from the girl who had answered his summons. Then he turned back towards Goade.

"I am not sure," he answered. "Perhaps I may hire another horse and drive through the night. And yet," he went on, after a moment's pause, "I know I shall do nothing of the sort."

He threw himself into an easy-chair with an air of complete exhaustion. There were faint purple lines under his eyes. He had the appearance of a man who had taxed his strength to the uttermost.

"You look as though you had been walking up these hills," Goade remarked sympathetically.

"I don't remember what I have been doing," the other confessed. "I only know that I am here and that it has seemed a very long distance."

"How far are you going?"

The owner of the caravan shook his head.

"I never know," he answered. "When I start I go on. If the humour seizes me I shall travel to Land's End, or again, the day after to-morrow I may feel like Piccadilly. To-night I have rather the fancy that there are unexplored lands in front of me."

"I should sleep here to-night and have a rest if I were you," Goade advised. "You'll find everything very comfortable. By the by, my name is Goade — Nicholas Goade. What might yours be?"

"I am Mr. X," the stranger announced. "I sign my articles — some of which you may have read — just 'X.' I enter my name in the hotel books — it excites curiosity — as 'Mr. X.' The licence for my caravan, alas, requires a larger amount of confidence on my part. I must confess that you will find inscribed upon my cards the name of Lauriston — Spencer Lauriston — a harmless name, think. Certainly not of gipsy origin."

Goade smiled.

"You're still thinking of our ridiculous farmer friend," he observed.

"Was he ridiculous?" the man reflected. "I don't know. He may have been right. My grandmother was a Spaniard and there were stories about her — one never knows. Parts of oneself may sleep for years and be suddenly awakened. Perhaps, after all, Mr. Goade, the farmer was right. Perhaps I am a gipsy."

"Your education ——" Goade began.

"True," the other interrupted. "I was at Winchester and Balliol. Yet, after all, there was that Spanish grandmother."

They brought him the sherry. He drank it eagerly, and watched the girl lay a place for his supper.

"A curious little comedy that into which we both stumbled," he continued, leaning back with his hands clasped behind his head. "A scene for a painter almost; the woman so terribly unusual, with her flaming colour, her air of disdain, the farmer — the old fool! — who had drunk the wine of witchery and married the strange woman. I wonder what the end of it will be?"

"A tragedy, perhaps," Goade ventured, "or a comedy. They are never far apart. The makings of either are there. It depends whether the woman's spirit outlives the bucolic impenetrability of her surroundings. If it does there may be trouble. If it does not she may sink into kinship with her environment. A toss-up, I should say."

"Are you married, Mr. Goade?"

"I am not."

"Neither am I. Perhaps we are wise men. A successful marriage entails a terrible assimilation — an assimilation which means death to romance. Here am I," he added, rising to his feet, "talking nonsense instead of eating my bacon and eggs. What a pity I didn't arrive half an hour earlier," he went on, as he took his place at the table. "We might have supped together. As it is, do not leave me. I have no desire for solitude this evening."

Goade lit a pipe and stretched himself in an easy-chair.

"I'll stay with pleasure, if you don't mind my pipe," he acquiesced. "I shouldn't think you often bother about an inn. The interior of your caravan looked most attractive."

"I found no common land between here and the scene of our little adventure," Spencer Lauriston confided, "and my manner of travelling, coupled with my complexion, makes me unpopular with all the farmers.   Nothing can induce them to believe that I am not a gipsy, and that I have not an eye to their poultry, their eggs, their rabbits, and possibly their wives.   Anyhow, I had a fancy to sleep in a bed to-night.   My bunk is comfortable enough, but a little cramped.   When I am restless, I find it difficult to settle down. . . .   What's that, I wonder — a runaway?"

There was the sound of a galloping horse in the street.   They both looked out of the window.   A young man almost threw himself from a great bay mare, all sweat and lather, and rang the bell of a house opposite — a clean, white-fronted house with a brass plate.

"A Sherlock Holmes," the stranger remarked, "might divine that that is the abode of the local doctor, and that there has been some sort of an accident."

The door was opened by a maid of neat appearance in white cap and apron.   The young man vanished inside, leaving the horse unattended in the street.   The latter, after a moment or two, crossed the road and came clattering up under the archway.

"A further effort at divination," the owner of

the caravan continued, "might lead one to the sup-
position that the rider of that horse was accustomed
to seek refreshment here. . . . We were evi-
dently right — a doctor."

Some green gates adjoining the house opposite
had been opened and a small car emerged.   A pro-
fessional-looking personage hurried out of the door,
dragging on his coat even as he took his seat, and
the car instantly disappeared.   The young man
crossed the road — a tall, stalwart-looking youth,
sunburnt and yellow-haired, but with a strange
drawn look in his face, and curiously set eyes.
Even as he reached the pavement they could hear
the sound of eager questioning voices.   Mr. Spencer Lauriston opened the door of the room.   The
landlady, an ostler, a waitress, and the newcomer
were standing in a little group.   They seemed to
be all talking together, but the note of their voices
was uniformly tragic.

"Has there been an accident?" the owner of the
caravan asked.

They turned towards him.   The waitress hurried away to the taproom to draw beer.   The landlady answered the question.

"This young gentleman here," she announced —
"Mr. Delbrig, the corn factor — he do have
brought terrible news, if so be that it is true.   He
have ridden from the Valley Farm, seven miles
from here, to fetch a doctor to Farmer Green."

"And no doctor ain't going to be any good either," the young man declared in an awe-stricken tone, his eyes fixed upon the foaming tankard which the girl was bringing out. "Right queer I do feel about it all. If ever I seed a dead man in my life, he do be dead."

"A stroke?" the stranger enquired.

The young man, who was busy drinking, made no response. It was not until he had finished the tankard that he looked around. His eyes were still set and glassy.

"Never had a day's illness in his life, didn't Farmer Green," he replied.

"An accident?" the stranger suggested.

"It's what we never have had in these parts that I can call to mind," the corn factor declared, his voice shaking a little — "it's just murder."

The landlady screamed.

"You mean to say that some one has murdered Farmer Green! Not his ——"

The woman stopped short. Some unspoken thought seemed to be in the minds of all of them.

"He has either been killed, or he's killed heself," the young man said simply. "I reckon the coroner will decide who done it."

The owner of the caravan turned back towards the bar parlour to find that Goade had been listening over his shoulder. He lit a cigarette and rang the bell.

"After all, then," he observed, "it was tragedy, not comedy, which was in the air this afternoon. Our friend with the violent temper must have been Farmer Green. I saw his name upon a wagon."

"The man," Goade added, "who took such a violent dislike to you."

The owner of the caravan shrugged his shoulders.

"He mistook me for a gipsy," he remarked.

A somewhat curious silence ensued between the two men. Goade resumed his seat in the easy-chair and, relighting his pipe, commenced to smoke thoughtfully. His companion seemed afflicted with a fit of restlessness. He walked up and down the room with his hands in his pockets, a curiously abstracted expression upon his face, his eyes almost unnaturally bright. Once or twice he muttered to himself. Finally he threw open the window and leaned out, gazing at a sign upon the other side of the way.

"The long arm of civilisation," he observed, "reaches us even here. A garage, I see — cars for hire. I wonder ——"

He turned away and left the room a little abruptly. Goade, after a few minutes, also rose to his feet and, crossing the cobbled yard, made his way to the smoke room opposite. As he had expected, the young man who had ridden in was still there. Most of the other habitués had rushed off homewards to tell the news of this lurid happening. The young man was seated in the corner with folded arms, and not all the beer he had drunk had driven for a moment that unnatural look of terror from his face.

"Is the doctor back yet?" Goade enquired.

"Ten minutes ago," the landlady replied.

"And the man Green?"

The landlady shook her head.

"It was the truth as Mr. Delbrig did tell us," she declared. "Shot right through the chest, he was. The doctor said he must have died immediate."

"Whereabout did it happen?"

"Upstairs in the farmhouse," the young man interposed, "just across the threshold of his bedroom."

"And Mrs. Green, where was she?"

"They do say that she were down in the dairy. Anyway, it were she who called out when she heard the shot and gave the alarm. It'll all have to come out at the coroner's inquest."

Goade sat down by the young man's side and ordered drinks.

"You don't think he could have done it himself — that it could have been an accident?" he enquired.

"It bean't so easy to shoot yourself in the chest with a double-barrelled shotgun," the latter answered. "Howsomever, if there was no one else to say who done it, suicide they may decide it was. Farmer Green were a man with a rare uncertain temper, and when he was fiery he were capable of any sort of foolishness."

"Are the police over there?"

"Six on 'em. They're trooping in from everywhere."

"No arrests yet?" a quiet voice asked from the young man's other side.

Goade glanced up. The owner of the caravan had entered the room unnoticed.

"Not yet," Delbrig muttered, "but if it is ordained that any one should be arrested at all, I reckon it won't be long. I heard the inspector say — and he be a powerful shrewd man, the inspector — that there wasn't much there to puzzle a knowing man."

Outside, the church clock struck the hour. The landlady turned down the gas behind the bar.

"Sorry, gentlemen," she said briskly, "you two who are spending the night here can sit as long as you like in the bar parlour on the other side, and Mr. Delbrig, too, if he's a mind. There's nobody will be harsh on him after the ride he's had, and Ned says the mare won't be fit to start again for a hour."

The young man shivered.

"I'm none so edgy on getting back," he admitted.

"Come across and have a drink with us then," Goade invited, leading the way.

Arrived in the little parlour they seated themselves around the table, upon which was a bottle of whisky and three glasses. Goade helped every one plentifully. The young man rose abruptly to his feet, wiping the perspiration from his forehead. His eyes were still filled with an altogether unnatural light.

"God, it's hot in this room!" he muttered.

He strode to the window and threw it further open. Then he returned to his place and swallowed half a tumblerful of the whisky and soda. The night air rippled softly into the room. The silence of the village street was so intense that they could hear the sound of a waterfall from the hill behind.

"Murder," Mr. Spencer Lauriston observed, lighting a cigarette, "is one of the remaining dramatic episodes of an existence which commences to lack variety. Take a murder such as this, for instance — in an out-of-the-way corner of the world where one could scarcely believe that such a thing was possible. I am not sure that I altogether fancy my own position. Our friend here," he added, touching Goade upon the arm, "is unfortunately a witness to the fact that some sort of a disagreement between the farmer and myself was certainly in progress when he passed. Very well. A quarter of an hour later I leave. That must have been, say, five o'clock. Supposing I drove up the hill for a mile or so, left my caravan by the side of the road, descended the hill once more, and made my way to the back of the farmhouse. I should have had plenty of time to enter it, conceal myself for a time, shoot the farmer, steal back again up the hedgerows, and arrive here in my caravan at just the hour I did arrive. It is an uncomfortable reflection."

"What did you quarrel with the farmer about?" the young man demanded.

"I had no quarrel with him," the other rejoined firmly. "It was he who took a very violent dislike to me. He seemed to imagine that I was a gipsy, and that therefore I had come after his wife. The man was a fool. Why should he put me down as a gipsy just because I.drive a yellow caravan and because much travelling has tanned my cheeks. I don't speak like a gipsy, do I, Mr. Goade?"

"You do not," the other admitted.

"Nevertheless ——" the man of the caravan began.

He stopped short. Through the open window, along the silent road which led to the village, they heard the beat of a horse's hoofs. The sound grew more and more distinct. A cart rumbled into the village street.   Lauriston looked out of the window.   The twin lights of some vehicle were close at hand now.   A moment or two afterwards it pulled up outside.

"Late travellers!" he murmured, a flash of curious excitement in his eyes.

The horse's hoofs struck harshly upon the cobbles, the wheels creaked and groaned.   Then there was silence — a voice — the door of the room was opened.   The farmer's wife, with a light coat thrown loosely over her rose-coloured gown, entered the room.   She flung it off as she entered.   More than ever one realised the beauty of her body, the restless glory of her eyes.

"I couldn't sleep there!" she exclaimed.   "I had to come away."

Spencer Lauriston shook his head.   He was standing up, one hand gripping the mantelpiece.   His eyes drew hers and held them.   From that moment neither looked at any one else.

"A rash proceeding," he warned her.   "Supposing one of us three — I, for instance, or Mr. Goade here, or our young friend whose name I have forgotten, who came for the doctor — had been the man whom the police were wanting, see how you bring the crime home.   A French examining judge would find something magnificent in this situation.   He would watch your eyes to see on whom they turned, on whose lips your kiss might fall — the. guilty man!"

She laughed across at him, and a challenge flashed out of her shining eyes.

"Why do you talk like that?" she mocked. "You are not afraid. You do not know what fear is."

"I am not afraid," the man of the caravan assented. "Come!"

She turned at once and followed him. He opened the door and looked back.

"Good night, gentlemen!" he said.

Young Delbrig, the corn factor, staggered across the room.

"What's this?" he cried wildly. "Mona, where are you going?"

The door closed behind them. There was the sound from outside of a rippling, mocking laugh. The young man flung himself against the door, only to find that it had been locked. He sprang to the window, but it was too small for him to push his way through it. Outside they saw the flashing of the lights down the street. Already the car was climbing the hill. Great drops of sweat stood out upon the young man's forehead. He tore at the casement until his fingers bled.

"And I killed him for this!" he gasped. "I killed Farmer Green, who had never done me no harm. She always swore if she were free she'd be mine. I killed him — and she's gone! Hell blast her! The Jezebel!"

He was shaking with fury, hysterical with an overmastering passion. Goade held him in a grip of iron. Down the deserted street, white now in the moonlight, came the heavy tramp of the constable and the inspector.

IX

"THE only fault I have to find with Devonshire," Goade remarked from the depths of a comfortable chair in the bar parlour of the Wryde Arms, "is its climate."

The local ironmonger, Tom Berry by name, appeared mildly puzzled.

"What's wrong with it, sir?" he demanded.

Goade pointed towards the streaming window-panes. For two days he and Flip had been obliged to suspend their wanderings.

"Rain," he declared. "Look at that! Two days of it, and more to come. Everywhere else in England the reports promise fine weather."

The ironmonger gazed out of the window, and scratched his chin thoughtfully.

"Us wouldn't call that rain," he expostulated. "It's misting like, but it don't do no harm."

"It would wet you to the skin in ten minutes if you went out in it," Goade rejoined.

Tom Berry smiled. He was a tolerant man, always willing to recognise the stranger's point of view.

"It dries off in no time," he remarked. "A drop of good rain water does do good to the skin and the body — freshens things up like. Too much dry sunshine breeds disease, they do say."

"I reckon Tom's right," Farrow, the local butcher, agreed, with twinkling eyes. "Sun makes dust, and all the doctor folks say that where there's dust there do be germs. Now, I should say there wouldn't be a speck of dust in Wryde come a fortnight."

"I'm quite willing to admit that," Goade conceded, "but you can't get about much in weather like this, can you?"

"It be good for the crops," Mr. Farrow, who farmed in a small way, observed.

"And it be good for us humans," Tom Berry added. "They be strong men in these parts, and I reckon the finest women in the West Country."

"What, right here in Wryde?" Goade asked.

"Right here, as you may say, in this small town," was the confident reply. "There's no one can deny that our womenfolk are something exceptional — famous too, many of them have been. There's Anna Craske, the schoolmaster's daughter — she was painted for the Academy. And then there were the Misses Drysdale of the Red House."

"The Beautiful Sisters of Wryde," the landlady remarked from the other side of the bar. "That's how they did use to be called, those poor ladies."

"Are they still to be seen?" Goade enquired.

The landlady shook her head. She was a middle-aged, pleasant-looking woman, severely neat in her dress, inclined also to some slight severity of deportment. She finished cleaning a tumbler, put it away on the shelf, and turned around again.

"There's only one left here, sir — Miss Adelaide," she confided. "Their looks have brought them little enough of good fortune, poor dears!"

"The others are married?" Goade asked, more for the sake of keeping the dawdling conversation alive than from any real curiosity.

"One doesn't rightly know what has become of them," the landlady confessed after a moment's embarrassed pause. "Miss Adelaide may have it in her mind, but, though she's a truthful-speaking person and an earnest church-goer, there are times ——"

She hesitated. Her embarrassment seemed shared by the whole of the little company.

"One doesn't count altogether upon what Miss Adelaide do say with regard to those sisters," Mr. Farrow ventured. "She's proud. All the Drysdales were proud. There's some as says that she doesn't know. It's a certain thing that that story of hers about Miss Henrietta having married a millionaire American was not, so to speak, the exact truth."

"How many sisters were there altogether?" Goade enquired.

"There were three in all," the landlady confided. "Miss Adelaide — she were the eldest; Miss Henrietta — she came next; and Miss Rosalind — she were the youngest. Miss Rosalind would be — let me see — thirty-two years old cum Christmas. Miss Adelaide must be nearing forty. Miss Henrietta, she was somewhere betwixt and between."

"Is there really any mystery about the two who have left the place?" Goade went on, stroking Flip, who had struggled on to his knee.

There was a brief, uneasy silence. Mr. Farrow was filling his pipe; Tom Berry was gazing through the streaming window panes. The landlady sighed.

"Some mystery it do seem that there may be, sir," she admitted. "It well might be tragedy. This bean't a place for gossip, as you'd find out if you stayed with us for a little time, but, if a power of talk could make it clear where those two have gone, there's many on us would talk from morning till night for the sake of poor Miss Adelaide."

Mr. Berry suddenly held up a warning finger. They all glanced at Goade significantly. The landlady leaned across the counter.

"Be careful, sir," she whispered.

There was a tap at the door, which was softly opened. A woman entered, at the sight of whom the two tradesmen rose at once to their feet, an example which Goade also followed. Notwithstanding the simplicity of her attire — she was wearing an unbecoming mackintosh from which the rain was streaming, and something which was almost like a sou'wester hat — there was a quality about her presence, her voice, a beauty of feature, complexion and colouring which would have made her a striking figure in any assembly. She smiled upon them all graciously. Her attention, however, was riveted upon Goade.

"You will excuse my trespassing, Mrs. Delbridge," she begged. "I heard that there was a stranger here — a gentleman from London, perhaps."

"You be never trespassing, Miss Drysdale," the landlady announced heartily. "Place a chair, Mr. Farrow. Will 'e sit 'e down a minute, Miss Drysdale?"

The woman shook her head. She looked intently at Goade, and there was an appeal in her gaze — a long, searching gaze from beautiful, softly shining grey eyes — which affected him curiously.

"I have most unfortunately," she explained, "lost the addresses of my two sisters, who left this place on a visit to London. They wrote to me regularly, of course, but my maid unfortunately, whilst cleaning my sitting room one day, destroyed all their letters. Naturally, not hearing from me, they have discontinued writing. My only chance of hearing of them now seems to be that some traveller like yourself may have come across them. The name of the elder is Henrietta. She is very like me. Rosalind, the younger one, has fairer hair, and her eyes are blue, not grey."

Her anxious gaze remained mutely interrogative. Goade was suddenly aware that every one was trying to make covert signs to him. He was quick to understand.

"I am very sorry, madam," he said, "but I do not seem to remember having met either of them. Now that you have spoken to me, I shall of course explain, if we meet, that you are anxious to hear from them."

There was a little breath of relief. The woman smiled graciously.

"That will be very kind of you, sir," she admitted. "There was a rumour — we heard something about Henrietta having married an American millionaire. There was nothing definite — nothing definite at all. If you will do me the kindness of paying me a short visit this evening, I will show you their photographs. I live at the Red House. Any one in the village will direct you. I am exceedingly obliged to you. Good afternoon, Mrs. Delbridge; good afternoon, gentlemen."

Goade was just in time to open the door. She passed out with a gesture and a smile which a queen might have bestowed upon a faithful servant. They heard her footsteps upon the stone floor.

No one spoke until the outer door had swung to. "That's poor Miss Adelaide hersen," Mrs. Delbridge confided. "A little touched in the head, poor lady — as well she may be, living all these years alone. A merciful thing it was that the gentleman was quick to take notice of it. She be easily hurt in her pride, the poor lady. There's never a stranger comes to the place but she doesn't ask the same question. They most of them humour her, as you did."

"The singular part of it is," Goade, who had been gazing out of the window with a puzzled frown upon his face, declared, "that I believe I could tell her where her sister Henrietta is."

There was a moment's breathless and incredulous silence. Mr. Farrow had paused in the act of knocking the ashes from his pipe and was staring open-mouthed at the speaker. Tom Berry had set down the tumbler which he had been about to raise to his lips, and had also become a mute effigy of amazement. Mrs. Delbridge was the first to recover herself.

"And where might Miss Henrietta be?" she gasped.

Goade hesitated.

"If I am right," he replied gravely, "in Wandsworth Prison."

The doctor came bustling in soon afterwards for

his usual sherry and bitters — a fussy little man who concealed a certain nervousness of deportment by an assumption of being always in a great hurry. He was short and unprepossessing-looking, but his eyes were both shrewd and kindly.

"Well, gentlemen," he said, as, carrying his glass in his hand, he moved toward a comfortable chair, "what weather! What damnable weather! A thoroughly depressing evening! I have just come from the Red House. I wish to God I'd never gone there a day like this."

"Miss Adelaide was in here half an hour ago, doctor," the landlady informed him.

The doctor nodded.

"So she told me. You've noticed no change of course, but it is there. As the body falls away the mind will weaken. In a year from to-day, if she is alive, she will be insane."

"May God forbid," Mrs. Delbridge exclaimed fervently. "Wryde won't seem the same place."

"If by any chance," the doctor continued, sipping his sherry and bitters — "by any possible chance Miss Rosalind or Miss Henrietta, or, better still, both of them, should turn up, things might be altogether different. What's killing her is the anxiety and this daily little torment of deceit. She's too proud to admit that they are deliberately keeping her in ignorance of their whereabouts, and all the time she's eating her heart out."

Goade found his thoughts travelling backwards. He was at the Old Bailey. There was a woman in the dock for whom things were going badly. Even now he could see her white face, her haunting eyes, the look she had cast at him as though in prayer — a look he had never forgotten.

"The worst of it is," the doctor reflected, "that one can't suggest advertising, because Miss Adelaide will never admit that the correspondence has ceased for more than a few days. A difficult situation! A very difficult situation!"

"And in the meanwhile," Goade quoted under his breath, "the patient dies."

That night, after his evening meal, Goade paid his promised call and lived for an hour or more with tragedy. The Red House was imposing enough — a fine Georgian structure, lying a little way from the road — but everything about it bespoke a bitter struggle against penury. The avenue was unweeded and the flower beds unfilled. Miss Adelaide herself answered the door. Her little word of apology seemed to indicate that the waiting servants had been outdistanced by her desire to see him. She led the way into a sitting-room, where there was plenty of good furniture, but a terrible atmosphere of gloom and disuse. Their footsteps sounded hollow, and Goade felt convinced that there was no one else in the house.

She seated herself on one side of the fireplace, and for a moment held out her hands to an imaginary blaze.

"I should like you to have met my sisters, Mr. Goade," she began. "They are unfortunately, as I have explained, both away for a short time. People miss them here. They are kind enough to tell me so often. I miss them myself. It is so foolish, too, that I have mislaid their addresses, and that all my letters from them should have been burnt. You are quite sure that you have not come across either of them in London?"

"I believe not," he answered, "but I should be surer still if you could show me their pictures."

She fetched him an album — an ordinary-looking little affair, filled with snapshots. In nearly all the cases the setting was the same. The three sisters were lingering outside one of the shops in the village street; they were crossing the road; pausing to speak to an acquaintance; entering their gate or issuing from it. Yet in a way these snapshots, some of them badly enough taken, had one point of amazing interest. The three women were the most beautiful he had ever seen together. There was in each the same graceful but assured carriage, the same long, supple body, the same perfect features and delightful expression.

"Why, you might almost have been of the same age," he remarked.

"There really seemed to be very little difference when we were together," she assented. "We lived the same lives; we had the same ideas until lately. Then perhaps there was a change; I have sometimes wondered."

"A change?" he suggested, hoping for some further enlightenment.

"I myself," she said, "was always content. Sometimes, though, I fancied that Henrietta, and even Rosalind, would have liked to have adventured a little farther into the world. Our morning walks, which to me were always sufficient, palled upon them at times. Their eyes wandered farther. Doctor Capper's greeting, Mr. Berry's rustic compliments, the smiling faces of all the villagers, their remarks that we could scarcely help overhearing sometimes, always made my day's pleasure. I think they began to want other things. They would watch a touring car passing through the place — a man and a woman perhaps, with luggage — wistfully. We came across shooting parties sometimes from the Hall. Henrietta and Rosalind were always a little over-interested in the guests. And then, as you know, the time came when, first of all, Henrietta went, and afterwards Rosalind, and since then it has been lonely; and, although of course I know that they are well and happy and will soon be here again, sometimes I am anxious. I should like to have word from them. Now that you have seen the pictures, Mr. Goade, is there anything more you can tell me?"

He avoided her eyes.

"Nothing more at present, I am afraid," he admitted, "but I should like to take one of these snapshots with me — this one, if you don't mind."

She cut it out for him with careful fingers.

"I should like so much to meet Henrietta's husband — that is, if she is really married," she said. "And Rosalind — if I could have just a line from her. If they could come back just for a day or two and we could walk once more down the village street at half-past eleven, to have the people look at us and say the old things, I think I should feel rested. I think the pains I have sometimes in my heart, that Doctor Capper cannot understand, would go."

For a single moment there was more in her eyes than should shine from the eyes of any sane woman. Goade rose to his feet.

"I must see what I can do," he promised cheerfully. "I am sure if they knew they would come."

"You are right," she declared. "If they knew! You must help me, Mr. Goade. You have the pictures. Henrietta could never escape observation. You will find her."

"I feel sure," he agreed, "that I shall find her."

Goade walked a little sadly through the empty streets back to the inn. Once under the arch, he paused to look out at the weather. The rain which did not count in Devonshire was descending in waves of irresistible moisture. There were puddles everywhere, a small stream surging down by the side of the pavements. He returned, thrust his head in at the bar window and demanded a time-table.

"You're not leaving us, Mr. Goade?" the land-lady asked.

"I might go away for a couple of days until the weather improves," Goade explained.

She looked at him a little dubiously.

"You don't fancy our Devon mists."

"I find them," he acknowledged, "almost as bad as rain."

At two o'clock on the following afternoon Goade presented himself unexpectedly in the office of one of his staff at Scotland Yard. He met with a good-natured but somewhat surprised welcome from a fat little man who sat in the seat of au-thority.

"Hullo, Goade! Your holiday's not up yet."

"Bad weather and a trifling matter of curiosity brought me to town for a couple of days," Goade explained. "Who's got the 'Silent Woman' case in hand — Mona Cross, she called herself?"

The inspector referred to a book.

"Jo Bates," he confided. "He's here now. Want to see him?"

Goade nodded.

"I'd like to."

A bell was rung. A burly, capable-looking man of early middle age presently made his appearance and greeted Goade warmly.

"Mr. Goade wants to know about the Mona Cross case," the occupant of the room confided. "Run it through quickly."

The newcomer nodded.

"Mona Cross, spinster, widow, or God knows what else, damned good-looking, about thirty years of age, living alone, small flat in Marylebone. A man named Jackson, a lawyer, not too good a character, found shot there one night. A neighbour heard the report of the gun and fetched a policeman. Woman never said a word; man appeared to be dying. The woman was taken to Wandsworth Jail. She never answered a question, never opened her lips. She's been up twice, but each time case adjourned; first time to see whether the man lived, next to see whether he was able to give evidence. The man was reported well enough to make a statement early this morning. I was going down there about four o'clock."

"Mind if I take it on instead?" Goade asked.

"Of course not, sir," the other, who was his subordinate, replied. "He's at St. Paul's Hospital, Ward Number 234."

Goade spent another hour at the Yard looking

up some records. Soon after four he presented himself at the hospital and was conducted into the ward in which Jackson was being treated. A sister placed a chair at the side of the bed.

"A gentleman from Scotland Yard come to talk to you, Mr. Jackson," she announced pleasantly. "You're feeling well enough to-day, aren't you?"

"Yes, I'm strong enough for that," the patient admitted.

The two men exchanged glances. Goade saw the wreck of a man of medium size, loose featured and with cunning eyes. Illness had at once brought out the worst and the best in him; it had robbed him of the grossness of too good living, but even accentuated a certain maliciousness of expression.

"You will remember, won't you," Goade began, "that I am from Scotland Yard? I may say that I am in a position of some authority there. I understand that you are practically out of danger now, and, as the woman in whose flat you were found has already been detained for some time, unless there is adequate reason for it the authorities feel that she should be released."

The invalid moistened his lips. He looked at the notebook Goade was holding.

"I can give you plenty of reasons for her detention," he said. "In the first place, the shooting."

"Don't hurry," Goade enjoined. "Let me have

a word.   I should like you to understand that Scotland Yard has your complete dossier.   You seem to have skimmed the edge of trouble once or twice, and your record with women isn't altogether a pleasant one."

"What's that got to do with ——"

"Stop!" Goade interrupted.   "I wouldn't excite yourself, Mr. Jackson.   That's bad for you in your state of health.   Just listen to me. Amongst other things which have come to our notice is the fact that you've been accustomed to do the — don't be angry if I say 'dirty work' — for a certain great man who lives down in Devonshire. . . .   Yes, I thought that might surprise you; but we know, and there's just an idea that your visit to Miss Mona Cross — she called herself that, I think — might have been on behalf of that gentleman; only unfortunately you let yourself go a little on your own account."

"She's been talking," Jackson muttered.

"As a matter of fact," Goade went on, "she has scarcely opened her lips, but some of her history has come to light.   Now, I am not speaking officially, but I don't mind telling you that I should like to have a statement from you to the effect that you found the woman in great distress, that your news was not encouraging, that she threatened to shoot herself, that you naturally endeavoured to take the weapon from her, as a man of courage would, that in the struggle it went off and you were wounded. Somehow or other, I fancy, Mr. Jackson, that that story might be good for every one concerned."

The man lay and gazed at the ceiling.

"Write it out," he decided, after a time. "I'll sign it." . . .

Goade, on leaving the hospital, was driven to an address in Sloane Street. A correct-looking manservant ushered him into a study of most luxurious and attractive appearance. Within a few moments a tall man, dressed with scrupulous care, entered the room. He looked at Goade enquiringly.

"I am Sir Martin Wryde," he announced. "What can I do for you?"

"I am Goade of Scotland Yard," Goade confided, "and I have come to ask you a few questions with reference to the shooting affair in Halsey Street some time back."

Sir Martin stood for a moment like a man turned to stone. Then he felt the detective's eyes upon him, and he made a violent attempt at self-recovery.

"What the mischief do you mean?" he demanded. "The shooting affair?"

"A lawyer named Jackson was found shot in the house of a lady calling herself Mona Cross, but whose real name is Henrietta Drysdale," Goade explained. "The lawyer was, I believe, an agent there to make certain propositions to Miss Drysdale on your account.   If you would prefer not to discuss this matter, Sir Martin, pray wait for your *subpœna*.   I will tell you at once that I am not here altogether officially, although I expect my position at Scotland Yard is well known to you."

"For God's sake, ask me anything you want to," Sir Martin exclaimed, throwing himself into an easy-chair.   "I'd almost be relieved to have the whole story blazoned out in the papers, and face ruin.   I've stood all I can.   I suppose Henrietta's given me away."

"The lady," Goade told him, "possesses that common attribute of all the most wonderful of her sex.   She errs on the side of an unconquerable fidelity.   She has never opened her lips.   Others have discovered the truth, and out of deference to her have hesitated to make use of it."

"Let's know the worst," Sir Martin insisted. "Here's my story: We were neighbours in Devonshire, and I swear to you that a more beautiful woman than Henrietta Drysdale never lived.   I'd have married her, but at that time I hadn't a penny.   The interest on the mortgages of Wryde wiped me out.   I was Member for the Division, came to London, joined the Boards of some companies, got a small job at the Foreign Office, and made good.   I'm climbing now all the time.   I ought to have married her, of course.   When I sent for her to come to London I meant to, and then

I thought — well, the same sort of thing that better and worse men than I have thought, I suppose. I lodged a little money in the bank. I sent Jackson to see her. I tried to make an arrangement."

"That's a straight story, at any rate, Sir Martin," Goade confessed. "I'll be equally straight with you. These facts have stumbled into my hands. I'm practically second in command of our department at Scotland Yard, and I have all the authority needed. Just now I'm on a vacation. I'd rather remain on vacation. I'd like to speak to you as Nicholas Goade to Sir Martin Wryde. I can get Henrietta Drysdale released in three days, on the strength of the statement I have from Jackson. Give me your word of honour to marry her and the whole thing's a 'washout.'"

Sir Martin rose to his feet. He came over towards Goade, and stood there with his hand upon his shoulder, looking into his face.

"My God, man, you mean that?" he demanded.

"I mean it."

They shook hands. Goade took up his hat.

"If I have any luck," he said, "you'll find Miss Henrietta down at Wryde in three days' time."

Goade waited for the next day before he visited Wandsworth, and then he took with him an order of release. He felt almost a little shock when the matron brought the so-called Mona Cross into the dingy waiting-room. Her beauty took his breath away, though it was the beauty of a dead face. She smiled at him gently, but said nothing.

"Not a word," the matron told him, "has passed her lips since she came."

"If you will leave us alone," Goade promised, "she will speak to me."

"It's slightly against the regulations," the matron demurred.

Goade showed her the order of release.

"The affair is finished," he said. "The man who was shot admits that he was struggling to get the revolver away from her."

Henrietta Drysdale started ever so slightly. As the door was closed she looked at him. It was then for the first time for two months she broke silence.

"But that is not true," she exclaimed.

"It is going to be true," Goade assured her. "Jackson has sworn it and signed the statement. He did it to save himself worse trouble. It may not be the truth, but it is justice."

"Who are you and how do you know anything about it?" she demanded.

"It is a long story. All the same, I bring you good news. Let me look at you."

"Look at me?" she repeated wonderingly. He took her by the hands.

"Henrietta Drysdale," he said, "I like your face. I see the right things in it. Are you great enough to forgive?"

"I think," she sighed, "that all women can do that — even too easily."

"Will you forgive Sir Martin, and marry him?"

She began to tremble. Then those eyes which had seemed wonderful to him before grew more wonderful as the tears shone in them.

"I don't need to press that," he continued, "but there is something even more important: your sister — Adelaide — she is losing her mind. The solitude has sapped her health. You must go back to her to-morrow, or the day after. Sir Martin will come down there in search of you."

"But who are you?" she demanded again.

He waved the question away.

"And now," he said — "Rosalind?"

The woman shivered.

"I am afraid to think," she muttered. "It was my fault too. Rosalind was younger than I."

"Is it too late?" he asked.

"Not unless she has starved to death," Henrietta replied. "Rosalind is prouder even than I — prouder even than Adelaide. She lived in rooms apart from me, because Martin was so terrified that she might see him at my flat. She was trying to get on the stage."

"Give me her address," he begged.

She scribbled on the back of an envelope which he placed before her. He thrust it into his pocket and took up his hat.

"But who are you?" she asked once more, as he turned towards the door.

"Well," he answered good-humouredly, "for a few weeks I am nobody. I am a man on a vacation in Devonshire with a Ford car and a little dog. I got tired of waiting for fine weather, so, you see, for a day or two I came to town and am making a busy-body of myself. We shall meet in Wryde."

He laid an envelope upon the table.

"Money for your journey," he announced. "It comes from Adelaide."

His other call threatened to be the most tragic of the three. His face fell as he noted the character of the neighbourhood, received the effusive greeting of a yellow-haired landlady, mounted the narrow stairway, with its tattered strip of carpet and stuffy odours, climbed higher and higher, until he reached the fifth floor and knocked at a plain deal door. A choked voice bade him come in, and he at once entered. There was no furniture in the room, beyond a plain iron bedstead and a washstand, hooks in the wall and one cane chair, obviously unsafe. From her knees before a small trunk which she had been packing there arose the third of the "Beautiful Sisters of Wryde", and as he saw her Goade gasped.

"My God!" he exclaimed. "How beautiful you are!"

A faint flush came into her cheeks.

"Who are you?" she asked coldly.

"A friend," he assured her.

"God knows I need one!" she cried passionately.

"Where are you going with that?" he enquired, pointing to the trunk.

"To hell," she answered.

"I will accept the allegory," he observed pleasantly, "but to what particular part of it?"

"I am going out with a touring company to Blackpool, under the direction of Mr. Montague Massen," she confided bitterly. "If you know Mr. Montague Massen you will know what that means. If you do not you must accept what I tell you — that I am going to hell."

"It appears to me, then," he remarked, "that I am just in time."

She looked at him earnestly.

"Surely you are a stranger!"

"Not a bit of it," he rejoined. "I am an old friend of your sister Adelaide, and a new one of your sister Henrietta. I was in Wryde itself forty-eight hours ago. I shall be there again within a few days. You will be there before then. Here," he went on, laying another envelope upon the table, "is money for your bill — I am sure the landlady will want you to pay before you leave — your expenses down to Wryde, and," he added apologetically — "a new gown."

She sat down upon the bed, her hands flat on each side of her.

"What do you mean?" she demanded.

"I mean," he explained, "that I am the sort of person who drops down from the clouds now and then — sent to straighten things out, you know! You needn't really believe in me unless you want to. Now seriously, please, Miss Rosalind — are you listening?"

"Yes," she whispered. "And I do want to believe in you!"

"Your sister Adelaide is the most tragic figure on earth. She has gone half out of her mind and thinks that she has just lost your addresses for a time. She has no idea that either of you has met with any trouble. You must both of you return, not as penitents, but in triumph. Will you please go down to Wryde to-morrow?"

"Of course," the girl half sobbed. "Is there anything in the world which could be more wonderful than to be back in the Red House in peace and safety. I'd go as scullery maid to the Wryde Arms rather than face what I have faced here."

"I don't think you'll need to do that," he assured her. "You will go back to-morrow by the eleven o'clock train. Your sister Henrietta will be there the next day."

"Do you mean that they are going to set her free?" she faltered.

"Not only that," he replied, "but Sir Martin is going to marry her. I can leave you safely, can I? You give me your word to catch the eleven o'clock train to-morrow? You'll find all the money you need in that envelope."

"Oh, I promise, but you must tell me who you are? What am I to say? You know what you have saved me from. You know what there is here throbbing in my heart."

Her lips were trembling. Goade himself suddenly felt a queer sensation. He caught up his hat. Nothing so absurd had ever happened to him. Nevertheless, he bent his head very low as he kissed her fingers.

"My dear," he said, "I am just a man on a vacation with a little dog and a crazy car, held up by wet weather. So, as I told your sister, I became a busybody. You won't fail me to-morrow?"

"Fail you!" she repeated passionately. "Never!"

Three days later the mists had all rolled away. The sun shone down on the red-roofed, picturesque little town of Wryde. It was half-past eleven, and there was the usual mid-morning stir in the quiet, clean streets. The gates of the Red House were thrown open and the three sisters emerged. Miss Adelaide, bearing herself proudly as ever, walked in the middle. On her left was Henrietta; on her right Rosalind. The roadman hastened to close the gates after them, taking off his hat with a flourish. Mr. Berry, the ironmonger, hurried from behind the counter to be seen standing on the threshold of his shop as they passed. Mr. Farrow, steel in hand, hastened out on to the pavement.

"Good morning, Mr. Berry," Adelaide said graciously. "We are coming in to see you presently, when we have done our shopping with Mr. Farrow."

"I shall be proud to see you, madam and ladies," Mr. Berry declared. "Wryde is itself again now."

Adelaide was all smiles. Rosalind lingered behind for a moment — there was a speck of dust in her eye; Henrietta stooped to pick up a handkerchief which she had dropped. Then they moved on. The doctor from across the street waved his hand; the veterinary surgeon, riding a young horse, was just able to control it sufficiently to take off his hat and venture upon a word of welcome. Mr. Sparrow, the tailor, with his tape measure still about his shoulders, came timidly forward to make his bows. From the snug bar parlour Mrs. Delbridge hurried to the courtyard in time to drop her curtsey.

"You see," Adelaide pointed out with triumph, "how glad every one is that you two have come back. There's Mr. Farrow getting ready for us. You must choose carefully this morning, Henrietta, as Martin is coming to lunch."

A battered Ford car came wheezing up the village hill. By the side of the man at the wheel was a small white dog. Then, for a moment, two of the "Beautiful Sisters of Wryde" faltered in that graceful progress. They moved out towards the middle of the street. Goade descended. He, too, joined in the homage. With an instinct un-English, yet which seemed suddenly natural to him, he bent low over their fingers, hat in hand.

"You know this gentleman, my dears?" Adelaide enquired, shaking hands with him herself. "But I see that you do. He was so kind to me when you were away, so interested to hear about your forthcoming marriage, Henrietta, so sympathetic because for a few days I had lost your addresses, and could obtain no news of you. Mr. Goade, you must really come and have tea with us one day — you and that delightful little dog of yours."

Nicholas Goade made his adieux and climbed back into his car.

"Some day, Miss Drysdale, I should love to come," he said, "but in these parts, alas! I am only a passer-by."

Then the "Beautiful Sisters of Wryde" went on their way; but one of them was feeling sad at heart.

X

THE PASSING OF JOHN THE HERMIT

SOME inscrutable impulse led Goade to choose the loneliest ways for the last month of his holiday ramblings. More than once he lost himself completely on Dartmoor and spent the night, to Flip's great disgust, in any sort of outhouse or shelter he could find. He traversed some of those great stretches of uncultivated land lying to the northwest of the county, where the roads have fallen into disuse, where an occasional blackcock, rising with a whirr at his feet, a lonely curlew, or a drifting hawk were almost the only signs of life. Late one September evening, with a boiling radiator and an engine knocking its sides out, he climbed to the ridge of the Five Tors and paused, almost as breathless as the car, to gaze at them — five lichen-stained, time-worn obelisks, standing around what seemed to be a pit. In the twilight they appeared ghoul-like, menacing, and Goade abandoned his first intention of scrambling over the broken ridges and bare strip of moorland to examine them more closely. There was a village, or rather a hamlet, marked upon the map, and he pushed on along the

road. He had a fancy that night for shelter, for
cheerful company, if it could be gained, for a ref-
uge from the storm which he felt somehow was gathering behind the blackened horizon. His road was
little better than a cart track, but it suddenly
straightened itself out, and before he realised it he
was in the hamlet itself. He brought his labouring
vehicle to a crawl, and looked from one side to the
other with an uneasy sense of the unusual. The
hamlet seemed to consist only of grey stone cottages of the humbler sort, a few on one side of the
road and a few on the other. Some might have
been small shops. There might have been an inn.
There might even have been a letter box, but of
none of these things was there any sign. It was
barely half-past eight, but every blind in every
cottage was drawn. Not a single glimmer of light
shone out from behind the curtains — not a voice,
not a sign of any human being. He made his way,
his car groaning and sobbing, from one end of the
street to the other, and more than ever it seemed to
him like some burying-place of the dead. Even
Flip looked up at him uneasily. She too felt the
presence of something unusual, almost supernatu-
ral. The place had no air of being deserted. The
windows were still there, and the blinds; only everything was closed and a grave and ghastly stillness
prevailed. As he neared the last of the cottages,
Goade brought the car to a standstill, left it by the

side of the road, and tramped noisily back down the sidewalk. Nowhere did he see a chink of light; nowhere did he hear the sound of curious fingers fumbling at the bedroom windows. He reached the last house on the left, and was pausing in utter despair when suddenly from inside he heard the low cry of a baby. Without a moment's hesitation he knocked at the door. The silence within was unbroken, yet somehow or other Goade, standing outside in the twilight which was now almost darkness, felt conscious of the near presence of human beings. Without hearing their voices, he knew that there were people gathered in the little room, that in a whisper unheard to him they were discussing his summons. He tapped a cheerful tune upon the window-pane. The door was suddenly opened a few inches — a little wider. He caught a glimpse of an interior almost Hogarth-like in its vivid intensity. A log fire was burning on an open stove fireplace; an old man was sitting looking into it and mumbling to himself; there were two women, a girl and a baby, a youth and a man of middle age in rough labourer's clothes, who looked out at him half menacingly, half with fear.

"Sorry to disturb you," Goade apologised, "but what's the matter with this place? I've been from one end to the other and can't see a light. Is there an inn here?"

"An inn?" the man of middle age repeated, his

voice shaking a little. "Up here, in High Tors? Noa, there bean't no inn. Who be'e?"

"A traveller," Goade replied — "a tourist, if you like. I've lost my way. Can I come in for a moment?"

Flip slipped past him and curled herself up in front of the fire. The old man leaned forward, and his eyes seemed to be starting out of his head.

"It be a leetle white dog," he said. "My, her's fat!"

Flip opened one eye, looked at him for a moment, and rolled over upon her back to enjoy the delicious warmth. One of the women turned around.

"Shut the door, Tom," she ordered. "Look at the sky, thou idiot. The moon's most over the Lesser Tor."

Uninvited, Goade stepped forward; the door was closed; he was inside. The youth pushed a decrepit oak chair towards him.

"Sit 'e down," he invited. "Ye'll have to stop now."

Goade looked about him, seeking for the most intelligent face. There was a girl there about sixteen years old, burnt brown with the sun, darker of hair and eyes than the others. Her hands and face and her slight, early stoop spoke of labour in the fields.

"Why is every one shutting themselves indoors?" Goade asked. "And can I buy some of that food?"

he added, pointing to a basket half covered by a coarse cloth, in which was a loaf of bread, some fruit, two uncooked rabbits, and a packet which might have contained tea.

The girl for some unknown reason seemed shocked at the question.

"That's not for sale," she said. "I don't know if there's anything you can have. We don't eat much to-night. There's a bit of cold bacon."

"Get 'im, thick-en," the old woman muttered, without turning her head from the window.

"If you have some water," Goade went on, "I have whisky in my pocket."

The old man at the fire looked up.

"Whisky!" he exclaimed, his voice shaking with excitement. "Cum twelve months last Christmas I'd a sup o' whisky. Set him summat to eat, Rachel. He's well indoors."

"But why am I well indoors?" Goade demanded. "Why is Grandmother there listening at the window? Why are you all behaving as though the plague was upon you?"

"You're furrin to these parts, 'tis clear," the man who had admitted him said. "This is the night when the September moon crawls over the Lesser Tor — the night when Black John comes down."

"And who the devil is Black John?"

There was a moment's silence.

"He be furrin to these parts," the woman repeated, half under her breath.

The girl in a rough way had laid the table. She brought a pitcher of water, and Goade produced his whisky flask. He seated himself. There was a strip of cheese, a fragment of bacon, some stale bread, and a dish of apples.

"Give me a glass for Granfer, and I'll give him some whisky," he announced.

The old man tapped impatiently with his stick.

"Quick, Rachel — quick, before the trumpet do blow."

Goade poured him out some whisky. The girl filled the tumbler with water and gave it to him. The old man clutched it with both hands and lifted it greedily to his mouth.

"May I know, please," Goade begged the girl, "who Black John is, and why we must all sit here without a lamp, and why Black John is coming here, and what he's going to do when he does come?"

The girl's features were unexpressive, but something like awe for a moment gave them life.

"Black John be him they call John the Hermit," she explained. "He lives in a hole in the ground up by the Five Tors. Once a year he comes down. He walks through the village, and what he wants he takes."

The old man had been noisily sipping the whisky. He still clutched the tumbler with both hands.

"He be a man of God," he volunteered.

"And is that basketful of things for him?"

"Sure-ly," the woman answered. "When the trumpet blows we lay it down outside."

"And does every one else in the village do the same?"

"Prutty well," the woman acknowledged. "Each gives summat. We talk together before'and, to get the things different. As he passes through he shouts the Word of God to our ears, he takes what's given, and, if there's any special message or any special house to visit, for a moment we see him. Then when he's gathered all up he goes; and for a year you may tramp the hills, you may search the valleys, you may wander wherever the fancy takes 'e, but no sign will 'e see of Black John. They do say that for them months he lives with them as ain't human."

"Well, I've heard some quaint stories in these parts," Goade muttered, half to himself, "but this is the quaintest."

All the time the old man was sipping his whisky and water with long, gurgling breaths. He leaned across towards Goade.

"Two years agone," he recounted, "there was a fine showing for him when he cum. The harvests had been good and a great year it had been for the 'tatoes; and, when he'd helped himself to all he'd a fancy for, he stood in the middle of the street and he cried out in the words of the Book that the gift of continency had passed from him, and that he maun take a wife. The maidens they were scared, and they lay still as the hares in the bracken before a storm, but he took Garge Dunbridge's darter — tuk her away wi' him up to the Tors, and her so scared that she did nothing but moan like."

"What happened to her?" Goade asked.

There was a moment's silence. The old man took a long and noisy sip of his drink.

"She cum back to have her baby," he replied, "but not a word would she say. She died wi'out a word. She were like a wild thing."

There was a quality of awe in the silence which prevailed. Goade caught once more an expression in the face of the girl. She was shivering from head to foot. Her black eyes were filled with a nameless dread. Even whilst they spoke she crept into the shadows of the room. Suddenly the tenseness passed. There was a breath of relief from every one. Goade, keenly interested, left his chair and moved nearer to the window. The stillness outside was broken in a strange and thrilling fashion — by a single, long note, which might have been from a reed pipe or a trumpet — some melancholy, homemade instrument, with a long minor call, sweet yet compelling. As it died away a man's voice rang out — a voice of tremendous volume, yet not without quality.

"Listen all ye who wait, for ye know not at what hour the Redeemer cometh."

There was instantly a queer sound as of the fluttering of wings. The blinds of every house in the village seemed for a moment to be lifted. Out on the sidewalk were heaped the offerings. Then silence again, and the voice, nearer this time.

"The angel of the Lord comes like a thief in the night. Listen, for all ye may hear, from the hills is the sound as of footsteps upon wool. Nearer, nearer, nearer they come. Sinners, incline your ears, and ye watchers of the night. The heavens have opened and the truth has gone forth. The Day of Judgment is at hand."

The younger woman began to sob. The girl in the far corner was shaking with fear. The old man inclined his head.

"That's him," he muttered. "He's at one with the Lord. Stand away from the window, stranger. He must see no shadow upon the blind as he passes by."

The footsteps outside grew nearer. Goade, notwithstanding a natural vein of materialism, found himself drawn to some extent into the outer edges of the maelstrom of strange, unreasoning excitement with which all the little company seemed imbued. The footsteps of the man and the pattering hoofs of the donkey were now clearly audible. When they paused almost outside, a little shiver

passed through the womenkind. The old grandmother was shaking like a leaf; the girl had drawn
so far back into the corner that only her dark eyes
were visible, coupled with which the sound of her
hurried breathing alone betrayed her presence.
Then the voice of the man rang out once more —
this time only a few feet from the window, resonant,
almost triumphant.

"Is it thus you treat the Servant of the Lord
God, O ye of little faith? I asked for bread and ye
gave me a stone."

There was a fearsome silence. Then the old
woman spoke with quavering voice.

"I knew he wouldn't like them rabbits."

No one else uttered a sound. Then the footsteps
were heard again. The door was opened, and,
stooping low, the huge form of a man entered. He
closed the door behind him and stood upright — a
giant of six feet and a half in height, long and hard,
lean of face, black-bearded and black-haired, his
head nearly touching the ceiling.

"Let there be light," he ordered.

The man of the family lit a candle. The great,
horny fingers trembled as he struck the match. The
newcomer lifted the candle over his head and gazed
across the room to where the girl was shrinking
back.

"Come ye," he cried, "to be the hand-maiden of
the Lord. Thou art chosen above all others."

The girl gave a little wail — the cry of one who parts with life. Nevertheless, she crept forward. The man took her by the arm and led her to the door. Goade caught a glimpse of her face, filled with frozen terror, framed against the indigo sky. He stepped forward.

"Look here," he interposed, in words which seemed idiotically prosaic, "you can't take that girl away against her will."

The man turned and looked at him. From his eyes the anger flamed. There was something, too, of real and horrified surprise as he stretched out his hand.

"It is not for the stranger," he declared, "to raise his voice in the house of the godly. Whatsoever my will may accomplish, wheresoever my footsteps shall travel, it is the Will of the Lord which guides. Kneel and pray that your sin may be atoned."

They fell on their knees. Even the old man slipped somehow from his chair. There were seven of them all around him. Goade, with an exclamation of anger, started for the door through which the man and the girl had issued. In a moment he was stifled. The woman threw their arms about him; the man blocked the way. He was hemmed in on every side.

"You people are mad!" he cried angrily. "You will let a crazy lunatic like that rob you of your daughter, ruin her life just because he has learned the trick of texts and religious gabble. Let me go!"

He wrenched himself loose, but the man and the lad confronted him at the door: the man, a solid lump of flesh and muscle; the lad as doggedly in earnest.

"You're a stranger," the former said. "You've no understanding of these things. The girl's mine, and, since she's chosen, I say let her go."

"The girl's not yours," Goade rejoined furiously. "She belongs to herself. Couldn't you see that she was terrified to death. If you're her father, man, come on with me and we'll fetch her back."

"She's given to the Lord," the man pronounced.

Then Goade knew that words were hopeless. He paused for a moment. Behind him the old woman was sobbing and the old man snivelling — then the sound of his long, gurgling drink as he raised the tumbler to his lips. Goade braced himself. With an unexpected movement he swung the lad out of the way, closed with the man, who was like a lump of helpless flesh in his hands, and, with a flick of the knee and a touch of the arm, laid him on his back and passed out into the night. The streets were still deserted, but here and there the flame of a candle was flickering now in the windows. Southwards, by the light of the rising moon, he saw the man and the girl and the donkey leave the road and commence the upward track to the Five Tors. He hurried back to the car, took something from the tool-box, and, with Flip at his heels, started for the moor. Not a door was opened, not even the one through which he had issued. As he passed he heard a mumble of voices, the sobbing of the women, the angry growl of the man, yet no one followed him.

Goade made no undue haste, for he realised that the climb was a steep one, and the light was at first imperfect. A hundred yards in front he could dimly see the man and the girl and the donkey struggling upwards. The man walked a foot or two apart — a dark, gloomy figure, muttering or singing to himself all the time. The girl, with her hand upon the donkey, walked with weary footsteps, her eyes fixed upon the ground, her body shaking every now and then with sobs. Goade waited until they reached a little plateau below where the five monuments of stone were reared, and then, quickening his pace, called out. The man swung round; the donkey came to a standstill; the girl looked over her shoulder in terrified fashion. So they stood until Goade, holding a short stick in his hand, drew level. The moon, shining through a faint, drifting cloud of mist, gave a spectral clearness to the little scene. The man waited, sinister and motionless. He still stood a little apart from the girl and the donkey — something, as it were, detached, yet with a curiously dominating influence over both. It was he who spoke first, and his tone was unexpectedly composed. It had lost the sing-song chant of his progress through the village. It was deep and rich and calm.

"Why are you following me, stranger?" he asked. "What brings you — a trespasser — upon my hills?"

"The hills are common land," Goade replied, "and I have come to take that girl back to her people."

"The girl comes with me willingly," was the calm rejoinder. "Her parents have given her willingly. Who are you that you dare to interfere?"

"You may take me," Goade proclaimed, "as representing an ordinary man of the world. The ordinary man of civilised places does not permit a girl to be carried off to the life you are proposing for her, even though her parents are ignorant enough and superstitious enough to yield her up. Come to me, young woman. I am going to take you back."

As though in a trance, yet with a certain shining eagerness in her eyes, she moved a step or two towards him. Her captor swung in between them.

"I am a man of peace," he announced, "because the love of peace is in my heart, yet I tell you that the girl remains with me. Come a little higher

with us and I will show you her home. I will show
you the spot where no goatherd or shepherd of
these parts dares to climb by day or by night. I
will show you the spot no gabbling tourist knows
of, because no guide dare bring him. You shall see
the Tarn of the High Tors."

Goade yielded to what he afterwards recognised
as an absurd impulse. He walked on by the side of
the girl, and a little way behind them — bringing
up the rear this time, in case they should try to escape — came their guide. Presently, however, he
took the lead. They passed round a mass of huge
boulders, traversed the narrow edge of a precipi-
tous combe, and came suddenly through a passage
of overhanging rock to an amazing and unexpected
panorama. The Five Tors, some hundred yards
each apart, formed a circle, and below was a great
chasm, black at the bottom with stagnant water.
Its sides were steep and jagged. There was
scarcely a bush to relieve the hardness of the stone.
The man picked up a pebble and threw it down.
It fell into the water with a quaint, resounding
splash, and afterwards there was silence. Ripples
flowed away upon the oily surface.

"Near here," John the Hermit confided, "is
where I live. Near here is where you will die."

Without a moment's warning, with a movement
of amazing swiftness, he sprang at Goade. The
latter felt the long, lithe arms gripping his body as

though in a vice, and from the first he realised that death was very near indeed. The man's limbs seemed made of steel and whipcord. He wrestled at such close quarters that none of the ordinary skill which Goade possessed availed him at all. They rocked backwards and forwards on the narrow shelf which overhung the tarn. Even in those moments of agony, with the sweat upon his forehead, with every fibre in his body striving to resist the terrible pressure of those entwining hands and limbs, Goade carried away with him a curious impression of the amazing serenity of his assailant's face. There was no anger there, no passion; simply a stern, inflexible resolve. Goade was a powerful man, but he was at a disadvantage. He struggled bravely, making every use of his weight, but he was losing ground. Every sense in his body during those few seconds seemed to be vividly and keenly alive. He was conscious of Flip darting wildly about, snapping at his adversary's legs. And then he saw the girl, he saw the idea frame itself in her mind, saw a light flash in her sombre, hopeless eyes. She picked up a great fragment of stone and crept towards them. Goade felt the courage to withstand suddenly intensified. They were within half a yard now of the edge, and for the first time his assailant's face showed some expression. A smile of dawning triumph parted his lips. He seemed to be preparing himself for the final effort. Then the girl braced herself. He had stooped just a little, and suddenly her arm flashed out. There was a dull thud as the stone, swung with all her force, came crashing on to his head. His arms suddenly weakened, his eyes closed, he spun round. Then, as though with the last strength in his body, he flung himself at Goade. This time, however, Goade, prepared, met him with upraised knee, caught at his arm and jerked him round. They watched his body — a strange sight — rolling at first, whilst the hands grasped convulsively at the jagged pieces of rock and dead sticks of bushes, until it gathered speed, fall through the air from rock to rock, and finally down that last smooth wall until it dropped with a great crash into the tarn. They looked over, breathless. For a minute or two they saw the face gleaming white underneath. Then it sank. . . . The girl began to laugh softly.

"I've always hated he," she confided. "I've seed he watching since I were a slip of a girl, and I've knowed. Now he's dead, and God be thanked!"

Goade took her hand, which she gave him gladly. Exhausted, they sat for a moment side by side.

"You saved my life," he gasped, still breathing heavily.

"I am right glad of that, I am," she rejoined, clutching passionately at his fingers, "and glad I be too that it was I who killed him."

Presently they scrambled down the jagged path towards the hamlet. The donkey, without a word from either, turned and followed them. Flip, relieved of a certain amount of mysterious apprehension, trotted a few yards ahead, making periodical excursions in search of rabbit burrows. The girl had suddenly drawn herself upright. She walked with light and buoyant footsteps. Sometimes she crooned little fragments of song to herself, a song not one word of which could Goade catch. Once or twice she came and clung to his arm like a dumb animal.

"There's something inside me," she confided, as they turned the last corner and the sleeping village lay in the moonlight beneath them, "something inside me, that's rested heavy on my heart for years gone. I knowed he'd cum for me — knowed it always. Now he's safe. He'll never climb up out of the hole where he's lying. Us'll never lie shivering again when the Lammas moon climbs over the Tors."

They reached the entrance to the village. She raised her finger. As she stood against the stile in the moonlight Goade was amazed. There was a new light in her face, a new intelligence. She carried herself with the slim grace of expectant girlhood. Even her speech was clearer and more distinct.

"We'll tether the donkey here," she whispered,

"and make no sound.   Now, you do as I bid you. Take off your shoes and carry them; walk down with me on tiptoe.   We must be away before a window opens."

"I must take you home," Goade protested in a puzzled tone.   "I must go in and explain to your people."

"May the Lord have mercy on ye if ye say a word in this place," she warned him earnestly. "Outside there's others'll think as you think, and understand as you understand, but here John the Hermit was as nigh as 'twere ordained to go to God Almighty.   You let 'em think that you took me away from he, that John the Hermit lies stark at the bottom of the tarn, and they'll stone 'e to death."

The girl spoke with queer, convincing authority.   For a man of resource Goade was a little confused.

"Then what are we to do?" he enquired.

She pointed down the silent, moon-blanched street.

"We pass down yon to car," she said.   "Not a footfall, not a whisper.   It be downhill for four miles.   God send we travel that far."

There were times afterwards when Goade realised the immense selfishness of his sex.   It flared into being with his next words.   A sense of shame sometimes troubled him as he thought about them.

"But what am I going to do with you?" he asked.

She looked at him in frank but somewhat hurt surprise.

"What do you need to do with me?" she rejoined. "I be young, I be strong, all my days I have worken like a beastie in the fields. There bean't a farmer who wouldn't hire me, or a housewife who wouldn't be glad of the chance. All I ask of 'e is to take me a safe distance from where they'd tear the heart out of us'n. You're not afraid I'd be a burden to 'e?"

"I beg your pardon," he answered humbly. "I'd no thought of that sort."

So he obeyed her. Down the sleeping village street they crept and into the car. The descent was so steep that fortunately there was no need for cranking. Flip, at first a little annoyed at being deposed, curled herself up on the girl's knees. They glided downhill, and presently the engine commenced to beat. The road was rough but straight, the moonlight as clear as day. They crossed, almost as though in a dream, stretches of moorland, thin strips of pasture, up again over bare, granite-covered hills, on to a great open plateau which led northwards. The girl asked no questions. She lay back perfectly content. As they travelled on, little wreaths of morning mist hung over the marshes. The black of the eastern sky was

streaked with fingers of lavender and mauve. An
added freshness seemed to creep into the breeze.
Away ahead of them were some paling lights.

"What place is that?" Goade asked.

"The township of Wryde," she answered.

"Then we're jolly well in luck," he declared
joyfully.

Even at two o'clock in the morning they were
glad to see Goade at the Wryde Arms. They asked
no questions about the girl. She was carried away
to the back quarters, and Goade conducted to his
accustomed bedroom. At ten o'clock the next
morning, as he ate bacon and eggs and drank Mrs.
Delbridge's perfect tea, he began to unburden himself to his hostess.

"What about the girl I brought with me last
night?" he enquired.

"She was up at cockcrow," Mrs. Delbridge replied. "We're a maid short. It's market day, and
she fell to helping. She'd be rare and useful to me
for a bit."

"She is yours," Goade declared promptly. "She
is only looking for a job. We've had a queer experience. I'll tell you about it some day. In the
meanwhile I must go across to the police station.
Any news?"

"News?" Mrs. Delbridge exclaimed, with the air
of one who has much to impart. "I should say so.
Will you have the bad first?"

He nodded. For a moment his appetite faltered.
"It's about Miss Adelaide," she continued. "After the young ladies had got back, and after Sir Martin he'd been down and the engagement was all announced, it did seem as though she were the happiest woman on God's earth. Day after day, at half-past eleven, through the iron gates and down the village street they came, and all on us were glad to see them, I can tell 'e, and then, quite happily, without falling ill, without a pain, without a word of sorrow or grief, she just died."

"A wonderful end!" he murmured.

The landlady sighed.

"She were a queer body!" was her mournful comment. "Well, then, before we knew where we was, Miss Henrietta she were married to Sir Martin and off they goes to Italy, and there up at the Red House is Miss Rosalind all alone."

"Ah!" Goade murmured, pushing aside his plate and helping himself to marmalade. "All alone, eh?"

"And more beautiful than ever. If there's any sense left in mankind, it won't be for long."

Goade finished his breakfast and lit his pipe.

"Can I speak to my protégée, Mrs. Delbridge?"

"Were you meaning the young woman you brought with you last night?" the landlady enquired. "She's outside in the yard, waiting for a word with you."

Goade stepped into the cobbled yard. The girl came forward eagerly. Her face was a little flushed, her eyes were bright with the joy of living.

"Sir," she said, "the woman here would like to keep me, and I would sure like to stay. It's work I can do easy, and a happy life it would be. We're far enough away, too, from Five Tors."

Goade smiled.

"Bless you, child," he replied, "go to it! I'll see that no trouble comes to you because of Five Tors, and you couldn't have a better mistress."

There was one moment in her life during which she rose to heights. She suddenly gripped his wrists.

"I'm not a prayerful soul," she cried, "and words are things I be short of, but there's no night I'll not thank God for what you've done!"

She hurried off, and Goade paused in a secluded corner of the archway to relight his pipe. Afterwards he spent an hour with the police sergeant. Later still, he started for the Red House, but half-way down the avenue he met Rosalind.

"You!" she exclaimed, holding out her hands.

They stood for a moment or two perfectly speechless. Everything between them seemed to express itself in that eloquent silence. Then he passed his arm through hers and led her gently back to the house.

"I want to have one more look at your parlour," he begged, "where I sat with your dear sister Adelaide. And, Rosalind, I have only a month left of a wonderful holiday."

"A month," she murmured, a little breathlessly.

"I have squandered my time," he continued softly, "but not my money. I think I could afford a special licence. And then, you see, there would be still time ——"

They had reached the front door. She opened it. Everything was spotless as ever. As she led the way to the parlour there seemed to come to him a little waft of that sweet country air, of cleanliness and perfume, of calf-bound volumes, of precious things laid in lavender. She closed the door.

"Time for what?" she whispered.

He drew her into his arms. Flip gave them one look, trotted round, and settled herself for a long doze upon the hearthrug. She was not a jealous dog.

THE END